GREEN WITH ENVY

A Tea & Sympathy Mystery Book 9

J. NEW

Green with Envy
Book 9
Copyright © J. New 2023

Cover design: The cover Collection
Formatting: Jesse Gordon

Chapter One

LILLY TWEED was on an important mission.

She was the former Agony Aunt with the local newspaper, The Plumpton Mallet Gazette, but now owned The Tea Emporium in the town's market square, where she still gave advice occasionally alongside the health teas she blended and sold to her customers. She was also a partner in the exceptionally popular Agony Aunt's cafe.

Up until now there had been no direct competition since opening her tea shop, however she'd just been informed there was a new establishment due to open on the outskirts of town which sounded similar and she was concerned.

"Do you know if they're selling tea sets?" Lilly asked Stacey, her shop manager and friend. "Or doing any sort of outside catering?"

"I don't know," Stacey replied, shaking her head.

Stacey was an American who had come to attend the local university and get to know her father, James. He was British, but had not been in her life very much when she was growing up. Now, when he wasn't lecturing in London, he lived with her in the flat above and helped Lilly and Stacey in the shop when needed.

"We just heard there was a new tea shop about to open," James said. "And thought you should know."

"Thanks, James. Of course, you're right, anything that could adversely affect the business I need to be aware of, but I'm not too concerned at the moment." Lilly replied. It was only a small fib. The nervous fluttering in her stomach was a testament to that. "The Tea Emporium is well established and I'm sure my regular customers will keep coming back. Besides, we are one of the main stops for the tour groups when they visit the town."

"Exactly," Stacey said, nodding vigorously. "This other shop is on the town outskirts so people will have to travel further to get there. Everyone enjoys coming to town to shop and have lunch, as everything is within walking distance. It's a long walk from here to the other place and has no parking for a tour bus. There's nothing to do after that either. I'm sure The Tea Emporium will be fine."

Lilly nodded, although she wasn't feeling particularly confident. But she knew what her next move was.

"So it's part of the re-generation of the retailers near Luke Moore's butcher shop?" she asked. The plans were part of an initiative by the current mayor and work had started not long after she'd been elected. So far, it was going well. With the row of ugly 60s and 70s buildings getting a much needed face-lift and the older historical ones opposite being carefully upgraded to ensure the aesthetic character was maintained. The heritage of the area was very important, as Plumpton Mallet and the surrounding district possessed some of the oldest buildings in the country.

"Yes. This new tea shop is the latest. Are you thinking of taking a bike ride, by any chance?"

Lilly nodded.

"You're a mind reader now, Stacey? That's exactly what I was thinking."

"You need to go and check out the competition. It's not rocket science, Lilly. Dad and me will take care of the shop while you go and investigate."

"Oh, well, if you insist," Lilly said, grinning. "I'll probably not be back before closing. Will you be all right?"

Stacey rolled her eyes.

"Of course we will. It's quietened down now. Don't worry. We'll see you tomorrow and you can tell us all about this new place. Just leave the display stuff outside. I'll bring it all in shortly."

Outside, Lilly unlocked her bike and placed the contents of the basket on the pavement. When she wasn't riding it, her bike provided the focal point for the displays outside the shop. Filled with seasonal flowers or items relevant to certain holidays, like fruit and vegetables for the Harvest Festival, or Poinsettias, holly and ivy for Christmas. It was how many newcomers recognised which shop was hers.

Before leaving, she tapped the glass of the right-hand side bay window and a furry grey head popped up from the depths of a warm bed. Earl Grey, the former stray now official shop cat, gave her a piercing stare, as though not at all pleased at having his cat-nap disturbed, then yawned widely, revealing two rows of needle-sharp teeth. His head once again burrowed into the blanket to resume his all important snooze, his mistress forgotten.

Lilly smiled. Earl was another way customers identified her shop. It wasn't everyday you noticed a cat asleep in a shop window. She mounted her bike and set off. She had important work to do, too.

* * *

S O THIS WAS LILLY'S MISSION. She had been the sole tea shop owner in Plumpton Mallet for quite a while now and had an excellent customer base. But she admitted to herself, if not her staff, that she was a little worried the new shop would take away some of her loyal customers when it opened. She expected many would visit on opening day and the week or two following, just to see what it was like, but she fervently hoped they wouldn't swap their allegiance for the latest new and shiny retailer. She'd worked hard to set up her shop and make it successful. Sinking the majority of her savings into a venture she was passionate about hadn't been particularly good business sense, but she'd been convinced she could make her vision work, and she had.

The Tea Emporium was home too many unique tea sets that were exclusively her designs and fresh teas that Lilly herself had created. The premises had originally been a pharmacy, and she'd designed the vintage interior around the original floor to ceiling in-built apothecary cabinet. Once it held tinctures, tablets and powders for a wide assortment of ailments, now it held her precious teas for much the same reason. They were the lifeblood of her business.

Lilly had carved out her space in Plumpton Mallet, using her savings and the redundancy money from her former job at the local newspaper to launch her new business venture, and she couldn't afford to lose any custom. The new mayor was encouraging fledgling businesses to open up, and those established ones to help and support them. Creating synergies and mutual marketing initiatives to benefit all the businesses and, therefore, the town as a whole. Lilly was all for it. In fact, that is exactly what Abigail, her partner in the cafe, and she had been doing for a while. But they weren't in direct competition with one another.

Lilly grinned as Archie's voice, loud and clear, pushed its way into her thoughts.

"For goodness' sake, get a grip, woman. You don't even know what this new business is about yet. Stop worrying."

Archie was the senior crime writer at the Plumpton Mallet Gazette. They'd known one another for years, becoming fast friends during the time they were work colleagues. It wasn't until she'd left and set up her new shop in town that their relationship had turned into romance. Now they were officially a couple and Lilly couldn't be happier. He was her voice of reason, and he was right. Until she set eyes on this new place herself, she was fretting over nothing. Besides, there wasn't anything she could do about it, even if it was a carbon copy of her own shop. She should stop being so selfish and work out ways with the new owner, whereby they could help one another.

* * *

TEN MINUTES LATER, after some relatively fast cycling, well as much as her knees and thighs would allow, Lilly reached her destination and dismounted outside the row of shops. She wheeled her bike onto the pavement and had a look round. She'd not been to this area for a while and was amazed to see how much renovation work had been done in that short amount of time.

She hardly recognised Luke Moore's butcher's shop. It had received smart new cladding in birch timber, new paintwork, a larger display window and updated signage. There were also tasteful planters with Bay trees either side of the door. She glanced down the rest of the row and saw they were being given similar treatments. Whoever had designed it had managed to make it look historical and contemporary at the same time. It looked fantastic. Luke was with a customer but returned her wave and gave her a thumbs up. He was obviously thrilled with his new look shop.

A couple of doors away, a new book shop had opened and Lilly slowed down to look at the window display. There were two of Harold Evans' memoirs in the window that she knew Archie would love, and made a mental note to come back and buy them for him. She'd just moved on when someone bumped into her, causing her to drop her bike in order to re-main upright. She spun round and came face to face with a very contrite and apologetic looking woman.

"Oh, my gosh. I am so sorry. Are you all right? I hope your bike isn't damaged."

Lilly recognised her. Annabelle Haines was one of Plumpton Mallet's older and wealthier residents. While she'd never met her in person, she had read about her in the society columns.

Lilly picked up her bike and gave it a once over. There was no damage.

"It's fine, don't worry. It's a sturdy old thing. It'll take more than a little drop to cause any damage. I'm more worried about the pavement."

"Oh, that's relief. It's such a lovely one and I adore that basket. You're right, they don't make them like they used to do they? I had a similar one when I was younger. Much younger, actually. I doubt I'd be able to get on one now." Lilly smiled.

"I use it as part of my display in front of my tea shop in town."

"Oh, of course. How silly of me not to recognise you. It's Lilly, isn't it? I'm Annabelle. You have a tea shop, too."

"Yes, The Tea Emporium. Do you mean you have a tea shop?"

"I do. Although it's not open yet. Soon though. I was just looking at the front from a distance, to see if I could spot anything that needed improving, when I bumped into you," Annabelle said. "See? It's just across the road there."

Lilly turned and saw the sign proclaiming, 'Artsy Leaves.'

"It looks ready to open."

"Not quite yet. Would you like a tour?"

"Yes, if you've got time, I'd love to. Thanks."

Lilly grabbed the handlebars of her bike, and she and Annabelle crossed the road together.

Close up, Lilly was aware Annabelle's shop was bigger than hers. It was quite common due to the planning restrictions in the town centre. The size doesn't matter, Lilly said to herself. It's what's inside that counts. Apart from the shop sign, the outside looked a little drab.

"I'll be painting the outside before I open," Annabelle said, as though reading Lilly's mind. "It doesn't look very appealing at the moment. I hope you like the inside better. That's where I've been concentrating all my efforts."

Lilly locked up her bike outside and followed Annabelle through the door. She couldn't help but gasp as soon as she set foot inside.

* * *

I T HAD BEAUTIFUL TEA SETS displayed like Lilly's shop, but also had something more. Stunning murals on the walls and numerous pieces of art spread throughout the space. It made the name of the shop make sense now. It was a wonderful combination of tea shop and art gallery.

One of the murals depicted a field full of wildflowers swaying in the breeze. The other was Plumpton Mallet's town centre in years gone by. A horse-drawn carriage drew the observer's eye to the centre. Lilly was in awe of the talent and exquisite detail Annabelle had put into the rendition of the horse, carriage and the familiar buildings. She wanted to reach out and stroke the creature's mane.

"Annabelle, these paintings are absolutely amazing. I'm assuming you're the artist?"

"Thank you. Yes, they are mine. Art is my first love, and I thought the murals and paintings would give the space a unique flair."

"And you were right. It all looks incredible. It must have taken you ages to paint these?"

Annabelle laughed.

"Oh yes. I'd have been open far sooner if I'd just painted the walls magnolia! But where's the fun in that? Oh, do excuse me," she said as her phone rang. "I'm expecting a call from the electrician. Please, feel free to have a look round."

Annabelle had created a truly beautiful and unique space and Lilly couldn't help but feel a little envious. While the two shops were completely different theme wise, here was a welcoming space that she could envision people would want to return to time and again. She would have to up her game if she was to keep her own customers loyal.

While two of the walls depicted murals, the third displayed framed portraits, landscapes and still lifes. Annabelle had her own instantly recognisable, singular style and was obviously a prolific artist. There was one of the town market square in winter she would love to hang on her own wall.

As she wandered, Lilly noted the seating where tea would be served. Lilly would have loved the space that Annabelle had to work with. She would put in tables so customers could sit and drink the sample teas she made instead of sitting at the counter on bar stools. But she also had a prime position in the main market square, which more than made up for having smaller premises to work with. She gave herself a mental shake. Her business was doing very well. She should count herself lucky. She had plenty of returning customers. There were just a few changes she needed to make, that was all.

"Sorry about that," Annabelle said when she returned. "I've been trying to get some of the last minute wiring sorted out before I open. Most of it has been completed, but there's still one area that needs attention and now he says he's not available until the week after next. It needs doing before I can open. To be honest, I could really do without the added stress of having to find a good electrician at the eleventh hour."

"I remember the pressure I felt when I opened," Lilly said. "And how happy I felt when I finally ticked something off the list. Even though I added another three at the bottom."

"There are so many little things you need to remember, aren't there? I had no idea when I started this venture. Now all these small inconveniences are adding up and becoming a bit of a nightmare. Literally some nights. I'm waking myself up in the night shouting out my to do list."

"I know exactly what you mean," Lilly said. "And fair warning, it never stops, I'm afraid. The list of jobs to do, I mean, not the nightmares. There's always something needs attending to when you run your own business."

"Good grief. What have I let myself in for?" Anabelle said, laughing. "I knew it wouldn't be easy. But I'm not one to run away from a challenge. Quite the opposite, in fact. I refuse to be beaten."

"You've got a good attitude, Anabelle," Lilly said. "I hope it all works out for you and you find an electrician soon."

"Oh, speak of the devil. Here he is calling again. Fingers crossed he has good news."

"Fingers crossed," Lilly replied.

She waved goodbye and left Annabelle to her call. Unlocking her bike, she decided to quickly pick up something for dinner from Luke Moore.

A few minutes later, she was cycling back to her shop with half a pound of sausages in her basket.

Chapter Two

I T WAS THE NEXT DAY and Lilly had been working with James and Stacey during a particularly busy period. They'd both asked about the new tea shop and Lilly had said it was all fine, she just needed some time to think about some future plans. Stacey nodded, knowing it was better not to ask anything further. Lilly would discuss it when she was ready. Even James was keeping quiet about the new competition.

The day had run smoothly. Stacey and James had spent some time displaying the new range of tea sets and Lilly had been experimenting with new blends. There had been a good number of customers that day, so Lilly was less worried about Artsy Leaves for the time being, but it was still at the back of her mind. She knew things could very well be different in the future once the shop was open.

While dusting some of the display shelves, Lilly tried to look at her shop through new eyes to see what she could change in order to bring in new custom, but frustratingly couldn't think of a thing. She briefly considered displaying local artists' work much the same as Annabelle was doing, but quickly dismissed the idea. She'd probably be accused of copying, and rightly so. Besides, her shop was all about the health teas, and diversifying too much wouldn't do the business any favours. It would just dilute the brand she'd worked so hard to build. She needed to think of something else.

The door bell tinkled just as she was stowing away her duster under the counter and a man walked in with a young child in tow.

"Hello. Welcome to The Tea Emporium. Can I help you with anything?"

"Yes please. It's my wife's birthday tomorrow and I'd like to get her a tea set. Nigel here wants to help me choose one," he said, proudly gazing at his son and ruffling his hair.

"That's a lovely idea. Let me show you the new ones. Nigel, perhaps you could point to the ones you think your mum would like?"

She walked them through the display areas slowly and the little boy picked out the one decorated with sunflowers.

"Mummy likes these flowers," he told Lilly with a slight lisp. "We planted some in our garden and they grew bigger than me."

"Did they? Well, you must be a very good gardener. This one is one of my favourites. I think you've made a good choice."

Nigel's eyes lit up, and he looked at his dad with a big grin on his face.

"Can we get this one, daddy?"

"Yes, we can. I think mummy will love it, Nigel. Well done."

"Would you like it gift wrapped?" Lilly asked the boy.

Nigel nodded.

"Yes please. Can I choose the paper?"

"Of course you can. And you and your daddy can write the label, then we can stick it on the parcel. Why don't you watch Stacey wrap it up? She's very good at it."

Lilly and Nigel's father went to the till to pay while Nigel climbed on a stool and watched Stacey expertly wrap the tea set with his eyes as wide as tea plates. Stacey told him to hold down the ribbon while she tied it, and he giggled when she deliberately trapped his finger.

"Thank you for your help," the man said. "Nigel was in town with his class yesterday and saw the tea sets in your window. He came home very excited and wanted to get his mother one. I couldn't say no."

"I'm sure your wife will love it."

"Oh, she will. She told me. Nigel's secret whispers weren't as quiet as he thought they were."

Lilly laughed.

"Here's a little extra to put in with the gift," Lilly said, handing him a box of one of her exclusive mixed blends.

"Thank you. How much do I owe you?" Nigel's father said, reaching for his wallet.

Lilly waved the question away.

"It's on, andin the house. Just mention us to your friends."

"We will," Nigel promised.

"So are we giving away free tea with every tea set sold?" Stacey asked Lilly once they'd gone.

Lilly shook her head.

"No, I can't afford to do that. But Nigel was just too cute to resist."

Stacey agreed.

"I'll lock up now, shall I? We're due over at the cafe shortly for the monthly meeting."

Lilly nodded. Perhaps the meeting would give her a few ideas to bring in more custom.

* * *

ONCE THE SHOP WAS CLOSED DOWN for the night, Lilly, Stacey and James walked down the market square to the Agony Aunt's cafe. Having two successful businesses perked Lilly up a bit, but she knew she couldn't afford to be complacent.

She'd formed a surprising partnership with Abigail Douglas, the woman who had taken over Lilly's position as Agony Aunt with the local newspaper. When the paper had been bought out by a much bigger concern, Lilly had been made redundant as they already had Abigail as their advice columnist. Because she had still been sought after for help and guidance people were dropping their letters off at her tea shop, so Lilly had installed a post box at The Tea Emporium, which had angered Abigail no end and she became intent on making Lilly's life as difficult as possible.

The townspeople had backed Lilly, but after a bit of investigative work, she'd come to realise Abigail had some serious personal problems and wanted to help her. The result was Abigail left the paper and went into business with Lilly at the cafe. It was something neither of them had anticipated, but they were now fast friends and business partners. Lilly was glad she was working with Abigail.

When they arrived, the cafe was still open, so they ordered some food and told Abigail they'd meet up in the back event room when she closed. The sausages Lilly had bought for that night's dinner would have to wait until tomorrow.

They all chose soup and sandwiches, quick to eat and easy to prepare. They'd hardly started when Abigail arrived.

"Sorry to have kept you waiting. Fred is going to lock up for me so we can get started."

"If you continue to feed us this superb food, we're more than happy to wait as long is takes, Abigail," James said, to agreeable laughter.

"Shall we start?" Lilly asked to a sea of nods around the table. "First things first. Does anyone have any ideas for new promotions or advertising?"

"I thought about the summer and to me, that means peaches. How about a peach blend for the tea?" Stacey said.

"Good idea. I have some peach tea at the shop. Let me work on some blends and I'll get back to everyone in a couple of days. I'll also get together some peach based mocktails for here, if that's all right with you, Abigail?"

"Absolutely. I could do peach turnovers for the cafe," Abigail chimed in. "That would help keep the links and the brand."

"Great," Stacey said. "We could promote a peachy summer for everyone."

"I like it," Lilly said. "Could you get some mock-ups together, Stacey?"

"Anticipating your needs, like the great manager I am," Stacey replied with a cheeky grin. "I've already done a couple and put together a potential idea for the take away cups. They've become really good collector's items."

She swung her laptop round so everyone could see the screen. On it was a cartoon peach character laying on the beach, wearing a swimsuit and sipping tea. Stacey had made it look like an advert from the 1950s to brand it with the vintage theme of the Lilly's shop. Lilly and Abigail laughed.

"And you'd put Miss Peach on the cups, too?" James asked, smiling fondly at his daughter.

"I would. And Miss Peach is a great name, dad. I should do a Mr to go with her, and maybe some little peaches building sandcastles. Make it a family holiday thing. What do you think?"

"I think it works really well. Thank you, Stacey," Lilly said. "Abigail?"

"I love it. Well done, Stacey. What about a tiki bar some-where? I loved our stall at the winter market and it really helped boost both businesses. I want to keep that momentum going if we can."

"Yes, I do too," Lilly said, chewing the end of her pen.

"Especially with the new tea shop opening. We need to keep on our toes," Abigail added.

Lilly winced.

"What's wrong?" Abigail asked.

"Someone has the green-eyed monster leaning over her shoulder," James quipped.

"I do not, James Pepper."

"You do a bit, Lilly," Stacey said.

"Wait, a minute. Are you saying you're jealous of the new

tea shop? I've only just heard about it. How can you be jealous already?" Abigail asked.

Lilly sighed and leaned back.

"For the last time, I am not jealous. However, I do admit to being a bit envious. I went over there yesterday to see what was going on and happened to meet the owner. She gave me a tour."

"And ever since you've been trying to remodel your shop," Stacey said with a grin.

"Which you would never had thought about if you hadn't gone over there," James added.

"I know. But honestly, you should see the place. It's beautiful. It's one of the old Victorian stables, so much bigger than my shop. It's light and airy and she's done some truly amazing murals on the walls. She is also an exceptional artist and is selling some beautiful paintings. She was talking about showcasing and selling the work of local artists, too. Not to mention the tea blends that she's selling. It's like a combination tea shop and art gallery."

"Wow," Abigail said. "It sounds fabulous. No wonder you're jealous."

"Abigail."

"Sorry, I mean envious."

"Oh wait!" Stacey said, scrabbling about in the pocket of her jeans. "Talking of paintings, someone stopped by the shop earlier. I forgot to tell you. I wrote it down."

She handed Lilly a scrap of paper.

"Who was it?"

Stacey shrugged.

"No idea. But they wanted to invite you to be a judge at

this year's artist competition. Isn't that something that would draw favourable attention to the shop and cafe?"

* * *

LILLY WAS THE ONLY PERSON at the meeting who was a born and bred local, so knew all about the annual Amateur Artist Society competition and exhibition. It had gone from strength to strength since its first year and now drew artists from all over the country. Many of whom caught the eye of agents and galleries who wandered the event in search of new talent. It was a really big deal for their small town.

She explained all this to her colleagues as she read the invitation Stacey had scribbled down from the chairperson and organiser, Mable Standish.

"Gosh, Lilly, you really should do it. This could be the big draw we need for the business. Attracting new customers from all over the country is exactly what we need," Abigail said.

"I have every intention of saying yes, Abigail, don't worry about that. It's filled with people you'd normally see on the society pages of the national papers."

"We might get some high end customers wanting events from you being a judge."

"You never know. So, is there any more business?" Lilly asked. "No? All right, let's get cleaned up here and we'll call it a night."

They all parted ways outside the cafe and Lilly went back to the shop to pick up her cat. Once inside, he tried to climb her trousers and weaved figure eights around her legs as she was walking, mewing loudly.

"It's food you're wanting, is it, Mr Grey?" Lilly asked. "I think you must have been a hobbit in a former life. I know you had a second breakfast courtesy of James. But if you think you're going to get fed seven times a day, young man, you're in for a shock. We can't have you being overweight. But, I'll relent. Just this once, mind you. Don't think it will become a regular thing. "

She put some food in his dish and while she was waiting for him to finish, decided to work on the Peachy Summer tea blend.

It was times like these she felt the history of the former apothecary seeping from the walls and swirling in the air. As she mixed and blended, dismissing certain combinations that didn't work, time flew by. An hour and a half later, she'd found the perfect mix and shouted 'Eureka,' much to Earl's consternation. He'd slunk back to his bed in the window ages ago and Lilly hadn't noticed.

"Sorry, Earl. Come on, let's go home. I think that's enough work for one day."

Chapter Three

TWO DAYS LATER, Lilly was having lunch with the Amateur Artist Society committee. The other judges present were Mrs Elizabeth Davenport, Lady Meredith Gresham, and the newly elected mayor, Susanna Bates. The organiser Mable Standish was presiding.

"In terms of the catering," Mable began.

"Oh, I think Lilly should do that," Mrs Davenport interrupted. "Her food is wonderful, as are her teas. All the events she's done that I have attended have been beautifully organised and catered."

The other women around the table nodded their assent, except for Mable Standish.

"Actually, I was going on to say that we already have a catering agreement in place," Mable said, shooting Mrs Davenport an annoyed look for her interruption. "And they are doing it all for free."

Lilly was crestfallen. She certainly couldn't afford to cater an event such as this and not get paid anything. She'd really been hoping her business would get the contract. She gave Mrs Davenport a wan smile and a nod. Acknowledging her thanks to the woman for going to bat for her.

"Who has agreed to do it?" Lady Meredith asked. She, too, was a fan of Lilly's business.

"Artsy Leaves. Annabelle Haines' new venture."

Now Lilly was worried. Not only could she not compete with the catering quote, but if Annabelle intended to offer her friends the same deal in the future, then Lilly's business would be badly affected. She and Abigail relied on the external catering arm of their enterprise to help with the cash-flow for both the Tea Emporium and The Agony Aunt's Cafe. If that was cut off, there was no telling what the future would hold.

"But isn't Annabelle competing in the exhibition?" Meredith asked.

"Yes, she is."

"I'm sorry, Mable, but I'm afraid I see that as a conflict of interest. One of the contestants catering the event for free could be construed as bribery."

"I agree," Susanna Bates said. "It would be in poor taste. Excuse the pun, to accept her offer. Kind as it was. Not to mention the fact it would put us in an untenable position should word get out. Regardless of how well meaning Annabelle is, the competition needs to be seen as a squeaky clean affair."

"Yes. I understand the potential issues," Mable said thoughtfully. "In that case, are we all in agreement that Lilly and her partner Abigail should provide the catering?"

There were affirmative nods all round, so Mable turned to Lilly.

"Are you able to provide a quote now for tea and light refreshments?"

"Yes, of course. Can you give me the numbers and what types of food you need?"

Lilly and Mable worked out the attendee numbers and associated costs and after they'd both agreed to a figure, Mable wrote a cheque for the full amount, which Lilly slipped into her bag. Abigail and the rest of their team would be thrilled to have this job. With one item on the agenda dealt with, they turned to the rest.

"What are the main prizes on offer this year?" Mable asked.

The judges awarded prizes for first, second and third place in the various age categories, with the prizes being small cash sums. But there were also three big winners from the event overall. The prizes varied year on year, all supplied by local business in return for sponsorship marketing, and Lilly was intrigued to know what they were this year.

Lady Meredith took out her notebook and turned to a marked page.

"I thought the first prize should be the all inclusive four-day trip to London to visit the main art galleries, but Susanna suggested the one man show at the local gallery should be first."

"I thought perhaps an exclusive exhibition of their work would be more valuable to an amateur hoping to turn professional," Susanna added. "They get an excellent write up in not only The Plumpton Mallet Gazette, but the county papers."

"What are the other prizes?" Lilly asked.

"A large selection of art materials from the local art shop. A selection of art books from the new book shop on the outskirts of town. A one year subscription to ArtLife magazine, and a two day watercolour resident course." Meredith said.

"What fabulous prizes," Lilly said. "It almost makes me wish I could paint. What about the first place winner receiving their own art show and the trip to London? We could then divide the other prizes between second and third place."

"That's a big prize for first place," Mrs Davenport said.

"Actually, I rather think it's a good idea," Mable said. "If the first prize is as good as that, then it bodes well for next year's entries and attendance."

"I agree," Susanna said.

They all looked at Lady Gresham.

"Oh yes, I agree too. Lilly is full of excellent ideas."

They discussed sharing the rest of the prizes for another twenty minutes, then Mable moved onto the theme.

"This year it's all about the environment. We are emphasising a green theme. Protection of our planet along with the creatures that call it their home. That sort of thing. It's open to interpretation as it is every year, and I'm very much looking forward to seeing the entries."

Lilly was making notes to pass on to Abigail. They needed to encompass the environmental theme in their food.

As the decision making came to a close, and lunch was over, the ladies went off to their various pursuits. Lady Gresham to a tennis match, Susanna back to her office, and Mrs Davenport to the library. That left Mable and Lilly to finalise the menu.

"Thank you for letting me provide the catering."

"Think nothing of it, Lilly. You were always my first choice. However, as committee treasurer it's my job to watch the pennies, and when Annabelle offered to do the job for free, I couldn't say no. I didn't for one minute think of the potential conflict. Stupid of me, but there you are. I'm sure she will understand. Now, let us talk about the food."

Lilly turned to a new page in her notebook. She was looking forward to this event.

Chapter Four

THERE WAS A PALPABLE BUZZ of excitement in the air on the day of the Amateur Artist Society competition. Visitors had been arriving over the last few days. Booking into the local hotels and guest houses by the dozen, with more turning up on the day itself. Some enterprising locals had opened up their own houses, providing impromptu bed and breakfasts, with others renting out their whole homes and lodging with friends or relatives for a few days. Both the local radio and television would be doing a small segment. As well as the newspapers.

Lilly had managed to find a parking space in the main town car-park at the back of the shop, and walked over to meet Abigail and Stacey at the event hall. It was the same place where the previous mayor had held his fundraiser not long ago. Lilly sent up a silent prayer that this time, things would run more smoothly. She certainly didn't want a repeat of the tragedy that had halted that event.

Hung on lampposts, various banners advertised the competition and crowds were milling about outside and across the road at the railway station.

As Lilly was one of the judges, she wasn't able to assist with the food or the service, but she wanted to double check Stacey and Abigail were okay. She found them setting up the buffet table in the room adjacent to the where the paintings were exhibited.

They'd both been very secretive about what they had planned in terms of the display. Lilly trusted them to come up with something suitably original and artistic focusing on the environmental theme, but even she couldn't have envisaged what they'd achieved.

The entire buffet table looked like a woodland scene. The centrepiece was a three tier cake on a stand. Made to look like a segmented tree trunk, it had expertly moulded leaves running around the outside, with three squirrels chasing one another to the top. On a side branch sat an owl, and the main topper was a badger sitting with a fox. It was incredible.

Either end of the table were two large pots housing imitation silver birch trees, their branches arcing over the main table and hung with small fairy lights. The platters of sumptuous food were surrounded by linen napkins folded into the shapes of frogs, swans and rabbits.

Lilly looked at Abigail and Stacey, both grinning expectantly at her from behind the display.

"You two have really outdone yourselves. This is absolutely spectacular. Well done, both of you."

"We thought you'd like it," Abigail said.

"Like it? I love it, Abigail. I can't believe you've created all this in the time you had. I mean, that cake must have taken hours. However, did you manage it?"

"The cake was already done and in the freezer. It was just a matter of the decoration and that actually didn't take as long as you would think."

"Don't let her fool you," Stacey said. "She's been creating leaves and animals well into the night ever since we got the job."

"Tattle tale," Abigail said, smiling. "I loved every minute of it. In fact, I'm thinking of setting up my own video channel on-line to show others how to do it. With Stacey's help, of course."

"She'll be famous," Stacey said. "Then the tea shop and the cafe will be too."

"I don't know where you'll find the time, but it's a great idea," Lilly said.

"So, what are you doing in here, Lilly?" Abigail asked. "I thought the judges were all meeting in the back?"

"They are. I was on my way, but couldn't resist peeking at what you'd done. I'm extremely impressed. Make sure you take lots of photos for the website."

"Already done, boss," Stacey said.

"Of course it is. Well, save me one of those tiger cupcakes. They look delicious."

* * *

A S THE PREMISES ALSO DOUBLED as a theatre, Lilly found the other judges in the green room.

The usual format was for the judges to see the entries for the first time when they were critiquing, so Lilly had avoided the exhibition space. It was also due to be judged blind, so the names of the entrants were covered up.

"This is one of the biggest crowds we've had so far," Mable said. "And it's been going for years. I am absolutely thrilled at the turnout."

"I'm really looking forward to being part of the judging this year," Lilly said. "I've always attended the event and the entries seem to get better and better. It's going to be a difficult decision, winnowing it down to the few lucky winners."

"It always is," Lady Meredith said. "But I'm sure you'll do a good job, Lilly."

"I can't wait to see all the magnificent artwork," Mrs Davenport chimed in. "I can't paint or draw for toffee. I'm always in awe of such talented people."

"So, what are you looking for in a painting?" Susanna asked Lilly.

"I suppose the first thing is it meets the criteria. But it will need to speak to me in some way. Art is very subjective and personal, though, isn't it? That's why I think it will be so difficult to choose the winners."

Just then there was a sharp rat-a-tat-tat at the door and Mable went to answer it. Lilly turned, recognising the knock immediately, and spied Archie's grinning face over Mable's shoulder. He gave her a quick wink, then went into his spiel.

"Good afternoon, ladies. I'm happy to say I've drawn the long straw for covering the event for the paper and wondered if you had time for a short interview?"

Mrs Davenport took a deep breath, but Archie pounced on Lilly.

"What about you, Lilly? It's your first time as one of the judges and, of course, as our local celebrity, I'm sure the readers would be interested in what you have to say."

Lilly laughed and shook her head. Local celebrity indeed! What on earth was he doing? Archie was an investigative crime reporter he never reported on local events. Besides, everyone knew they were a couple. It looked like favouritism asking her first. But Archie sensed what she was thinking and went straight into his questions with a professional attitude. After a quick chat, Archie turned to the rest of ladies.

"I noticed the names of the artists have been covered. Can you tell me why that is?"

"So we're not accused of bias, of course," Mrs Davenport blurted out. Archie started at her forceful tone and Mable and the others winced.

"What Mrs Davenport means is that we have to judge the art on its own merit. Be fully transparent and not be influenced in any way by who painted it."

There was a collective sigh of relief as Lilly tactfully explained the clumsy response. Mrs Davenport huffed and stuck her chin out. She was clearly about to sulk. Sensing the tension, Archie turned to her.

"Mrs Davenport, as an important resident, do you think the exhibition and competition are good for the town?"

Lilly recognised the soft soaping and an elementary question when she heard one, and had to fight hard not to grin.

"Oh absolutely," Mrs Davenport began, her cheeks tinged pink with delight at Archie's compliment. She continued to wax lyrical for some moments while Archie scribbled furiously. Shaking his hand every so often to prevent cramp.

The moment she drew breath, he turned to the others, receiving quotes and useful information for his article, before putting the lid on his pen and standing up.

"Well, thank you for your time ladies. Good luck with the judging."

"I'll see you out, Archie," Lilly said.

Outside, before she had a chance to speak, Archie swept her up in an embrace and kissed her deeply.

"Good grief, Archie Brown. What's this all about?"

"I came over to wish you luck, but you'd already disappeared. I had to think of an excuse to see you."

"You mean you're not writing an article for the gazette?"

"No, of course not. Well, not unless there's a crime."

Lilly held up her hand.

"Not another word, Archie. I don't want you to jinx anything. Remember what happened last time we were here?"

"How could I forget? Don't worry, not another word."

"So, do you mean we've all just spouted our best lines for no reason?"

Archie laughed.

"We've got one of the juniors on it. See, this is his notebook."

"I should have guessed. It's far too new to be one of yours. Well, I'm glad I didn't waste my breath at least."

"Unlike Mrs Davenport. Good heavens, that woman can talk. Unfortunately, most of it was rubbish."

Lilly punched him playfully.

"Be nice. It's thanks to her I got the job of catering."

"Really? Oh, well, that's good of her. I'll make sure her name is spelled correctly in that case. And talking about food, I've just seen the buffet. It's a sensation."

"I can't take any credit at all. Abigail and Stacey have worked miracles. Listen, I must go, Archie, but thank you for coming to see me."

"Anytime. Maybe we can get a late dinner once you're through?"

"I'll need to help clear up, but I think that should be fine. See you later."

"Ciao for now. Be good. And if you can't be good, be careful."

Lilly laughed and returned to the room.

* * *

MABLE'S PHONE RANG just as Lilly returned.
"It's time," she said to the room at large.

They followed her out into the main exhibition space. The building was actually two that adjoined with the stage and a large floor area on one side and on the other, divided by concertinaed doors, which had been pulled back for the event, another large floor area and a wide upstairs balcony accessed via an ornate staircase at one end. It was here, both upstairs and down, that the paintings were displayed on easels and hung on large room dividers built for the purpose.

The crowd of people who had been milling about previously had been ushered into the other side to enjoy the food and drinks while the judges deliberated.

"So, how does this work?" Lilly asked Mable.

"Lady Gresham takes the lead and we follow," Mable replied with a smile. "It's as simple as that. We comment and discuss the entries. Make any notes on our clipboards," she added, pointing to the one Lilly had been furnished with. "And once we've seen them all, we retire to discuss everything and make our final decisions. Each group of entrants have already been whittled down to ten from the many we had. So there are only forty pieces of artwork to view and discuss."

Lilly nodded. She understood why Meredith was in charge of this particular part. She'd seen the list of sponsors and her name was right at the top.

"We'll start with the youngest group. 16 to 24-year-olds," Meredith declared, looking at her plan. "Over here. Then move through the rest in order of age until we reach the last one."

"Oh, what a good idea," Mrs Davenport said as they moved to the first display of paintings.

"It's exactly the same every year," Mable whispered to Lilly, eliciting a smile.

As they approached the first ten art works Lilly's jaw dropped.

"I can't believe these were painted by youngsters."

"Oh yes. The talent here is extraordinary," Meredith said. "It's not an easy job to decide on the winners. They are all so gifted."

"This one is interesting," Susanna said, indicating an abstract work, which on the face of it looked like a closeup of forest tree trunks.

Mrs Davenport pulled a face.

"It's not really on theme though, is it? It's just a lot of lines that you assume are trees. There aren't even any leaves."

"You're taking it too literally," Meredith said. "Come and view it from this side."

They all dutifully followed, and suddenly Lilly could see what she meant. There were gasps from the others, too.

"I've never seen anything like it," Susanna said. "How clever."

Viewed from this angle, the negative space took on the shape of the head of a woman with a crown of leaves in which nestled a bird. It was like magic.

"It's the artist's representation of Mother Nature and more than fits our theme, wouldn't you say, Mrs Davenport?"

"Oh yes. I can see it now. It's very good," she replied, her face turning crimson.

They moved on to the next, a still life in oils. A hand-carved wooden bowl of fruit containing an assortment of produce so realistic, Lilly felt she could reach out and pluck the apple from the canvas. They strolled along the display, each making notes as they went, then moved to the 25 to 39 age group. Once again, Lilly was impressed with how skillful the creators were.

Even though the theme was the environment, the range of subjects and interpretations was incredible. From a stunning sunset juxtaposed against a sea of tall buildings encroaching on green spaces, to a mound of rubbish where a solitary fox cub sat alone among discarded plastic and broken bottles.

"Oh, look at all the lovely colours in this one," Mrs Davenport said. "Mixed medium if I'm not mistaken. This fits the theme, wouldn't you say?"

The others wandered to the entry she was looking at. Susanna reached out and touched a lump of paint.

"I don't even know what to say about this. It's just melted wax crayon. It's more akin to something a child would produce and I can't see anything in it to suggest the environment. Or am I missing something obvious?"

"I don't think you're missing anything," Mable said. "The colours are gauche, nothing you would find in nature. And I can't see anything remotely connected to our theme either. It's a very clumsy and inelegant attempt to be something clever. But it's missed the mark completely. I don't know how it managed to get into the final ten for this group."

The others agreed and moved on, leaving Mrs Davenport staring at the canvas and looking crushed. Lilly couldn't help but feel sorry for her. She tried so hard to fit in and sound knowledgeable, but she, like the painting, rarely hit the mark.

They reached the 40 to 60 age group and Lilly's eye was immediately caught by a stunning rendition of a stag in the woods. It was so realistic Lilly swore she saw his tail flick. Above the trees where you would expect rolling hills and sky, there was a barrier of skyscrapers. Lilly was beginning to feel emotional. Humans really were ruining their home planet for all living beings. She was relieved they were nearing the end.

In the final section there was a large and long landscape canvas, part of which Lilly was familiar with. On the left was an exquisitely painted horse drawn carriage surrounded by old thatched cottage on a dirt road with fields and trees in the background. As the painting moved on, the surroundings changed to a cobbled road and stone built buildings with an avenue of ornamental trees. As you walked, it changed again to a tarmac road, traffic lights and a gas guzzling four-wheel-drive jeep. The trees were gone, and some of the quaint buildings had been replaced with soulless concrete blocks. At the end, there was no sign of nature at all. The original historical buildings had disappeared to be replaced by skyscrapers so close there was no room for any green space. Nature had been removed.

The other judges were admiring the amount of work that had gone into this piece, and rightly so. It was beautifully done and more than demonstrated the environmental theme. Lilly was wondering if she could be impartial because she knew whose entry this was. She'd seen the same carriage on the mural at Artsy Leaves. This was Annabelle Haines' work.

* * *

"THAT'S ALL OF THEM," Mable said eventually. "Shall we move to the green room and begin our deliberations?"

Everyone else nodded in agreement, but Lilly asked if she could just take one more quick circuit around the display. She wanted to double check her thoughts and make sure she was doing justice to all the entries.

"Of course, Lilly. You go ahead. We'll see you in the green room shortly," Meredith said.

It took her another fifteen minutes to wander through the exhibition a second time, and apart from one change, she found she agreed with her initial assessment. On the way back to the others, she decided to pay a visit to the ladies' room.

She opened a side door and stepped into the hallway. At the far end, off to one side, she noticed something lying across the threshold of an open door. She lurched forward and was horrified to see Annabelle on the floor. Falling to her knees, she tried to wake her but the woman didn't move. She checked for a pulse but found none. Annabelle Haines was dead.

As Lilly reached for her phone to call the police and an ambulance, she realised there were several people in the hallway. Mable had obviously opened up the room to the public again. They were all staring at Lilly leaning over the body and several were calling the police while others were recording her.

Chapter Five

LILLY WAS STILL KNEELING on the floor next to Annabelle when her friend and senior detective, Bonnie Phillips, arrived.

"Are you all right?" she asked, helping Lilly to her feet.

Lilly nodded.

"Don't you have a sarcastic quip to make, Bonnie?"

"Not really. But, when this is over, I'd like you and Archie to emigrate."

Lilly spluttered out a laugh.

"Thanks."

"Hey, I'm only half joking, Lilly. Trouble seems to follow you. I'm just trying to halve my work-load."

Lilly nodded.

"I'm sorry, Bonnie. I'd just finished making my decisions for judging the competition and came to use the bathroom. I just found Annabelle collapsed like this and tried to help, but it was obviously too late."

Lilly stared at the pooling blood under the artist's head, then turned away, her stomach churning.

"Oh, Good Lord. What's happened?"

Lilly and Bonnie turned to find Mable rushing down the hall towards them. Bonnie stepped forward, blocking the woman's view of the body.

"Who are you?"

"Mable Standish. I'm one of the event organisers and a judge. What's happened?"

She moved around Bonnie before she could be stopped.

"What's wrong with Annabelle?"

Mable's voice had shot up a pitch and Lilly realised she was about to panic. Bonnie stepped in front of her and gently took her arm, leading her a few steps away.

"Tell me how you know, Annabelle?" she said softly.

"She's a wonderful artist and a friend, well acquaintance, I suppose really. She's entered one of her pieces in the competition." She paused, looking from Bonnie to Lilly and back again. "Is she dead?"

"I am sorry, Ms Standish. Yes, she is."

Mable turned visibly pale and Lilly moved to her side in case she fainted. But she took a deep breath and looked away.

"I need to ask you a few questions," Bonnie told her.

"Yes. But what about the judging and prize giving?"

"That will have to be put on hold until I've finished talking to everyone."

"I'm sorry. Of course it will. What do you need to know?"

"Tell me who the other judges are," Bonnie said, nodding to a constable who whipped out his notebook and pen.

"Well, Lilly and myself. Mayor Bates, Mrs Davenport and Lady Gresham."

Feeling in the way Lilly moved to one side and watched as Annabelle was covered with a sheet by a recently arrived paramedic and the area designated a crime scene. The paramedics left to wait until someone had officially declared cause of death.

"Oh, my goodness. Annabelle! What happened?" Meredith Gresham cried as she and the remaining judges rushed down the hallway.

Lilly sighed. Obviously, word had spread fast.

"Poor Anabelle," Susanna said.

"How dreadful," Mrs Davenport added.

"Ladies, you can't be here," Bonnie said. "Please, move up the hallway until I can speak to you all properly."

Bonnie spoke quietly to Mable and a uniformed officer and Lilly saw Mable point in the direction of the green room. Bonnie nodded and turned to the rest of them.

"I understand you have a competition to judge. My officer will escort you all to the green room, where you can wait until I can come and take your statements."

Everyone except Mable, who was still being interviewed by Bonnie, began to follow the officer. Lilly glanced back and saw they had moved into the room where Annabelle had been found. She was torn between wanting to help Bonnie and staying with the others. But how could she concentrate on judging paintings when one of the artists was lying dead just a few feet away? But Bonnie had included Lilly when she asked them to go and wait. She supposed she had better do as she was told. If Bonnie needed her, then she would come and find her.

* * *

THE POLICE OFFICER remained outside the room so at least they could deliberate in peace without having the long arm of the law listening to their every word. That's if they could concentrate on the task at hand. Lilly wasn't sure she would be able to. Giving out prizes seemed not just inconsequential but downright insulting and disrespectful considering what had just happened.

The door opened and Stacey entered carrying a tea tray. She deposited it silently on a nearby table and after a quick glance at Lilly, who thanked her for thinking of them, left the room.

Lilly poured for them all and handed out plates for those that wanted food, while the others began to talk.

"I suppose we had better decide on the winners," Lady Gresham said. "People are waiting to hear the winners announced. Although I must admit, for the first time, in all the years I've been involved in this competition, my heart just isn't in it. Instead of beautiful art, all I can see is poor Annabelle lying in that doorway."

So could Lilly. She was horrified Annabelle had died. A picture of the woman's pale, lifeless face and the blood on the floor kept thrusting itself into her mind.

"What happened exactly, Lilly?" Mrs Davenport asked. "Did you see what she slipped on? And how she banged her head?"

"I didn't see anything. I was returning here when I found her. I was just about to call for an ambulance when someone else called the police. I'm afraid she was already dead when I arrived." Lilly paused for breath and glanced around at the sea of faces before her. "But I don't think it was an accident. I think somebody might have killed her."

"What?" Susanna said. "But that's despicable. Why do you think that?"

"Who on earth would want to hurt Annabelle? She was such a unique talent and a kind and gentle soul. It doesn't make sense. Are you sure, Lilly?" Meredith asked.

Lilly shook her head.

"Not one hundred percent, no. But she had collapsed in the door entry and there was nowhere she could have hit her head other than the door jamb. There was no sign of her having done so. And from the brief glimpse I had of the floor, there were no signs she's slipped either. At the very least, it's suspicious."

"Well, you're our resident sleuth," Mrs Davenport said. "So we must take your word for it until the police let us know one way or another that it wasn't an accident."

"I still can't fathom why someone would want to hurt her," Meredith said. "She was always a bit of a wild child. Hugely creative and bohemian. A true free spirit. As though her very soul was too big for the body it was contained in and longed to soar free."

"You knew her when you were children, Meredith?" Susanna asked, sipping her tea.

"Oh yes. We were at school together and our families were close. She settled down a little after marrying. But she always was unconventional. Dancing to the beat of her own drum as it were."

"Such dreadful news for her family." Mrs Davenport said, taking a miniature quiche from a plate.

"Oh, I've just remembered something," Lady Gresham said, putting her teacup and saucer on the table. "I saw Annabelle's grandson here earlier."

"Had he come to support her?" Susanna asked.

"I'm not sure," she replied with a deep frown. Lilly's ears perked up at her tone. "I understood that Annabelle had written him and the other grandchild out of her will."

"Really?" Mrs Davenport asked, leaning forward. "Do you know why?"

Lilly stifled a sigh and noticed Susanna nodding. Mrs Davenport was the worst gossip. She would have a field day with Annabelle's death, let alone this news of an obviously severe rift in the family if Lady Gresham was right.

"I've no idea. I was told in confidence last week, so don't anyone discuss it outside of this room, please. But I know nothing more. I was a little shocked to hear the news though, and wondered what had happened to precipitate such a response from Annabelle, who was generosity itself. However, it was none of my business, so I didn't question it."

"Why would he attend the art competition if she wrote him out of the will?" Mrs Davenport said. "He would have known she would be here."

"He must have been intending to confront her, wouldn't you say?" Susanna said. "He must have been quite angry at losing his inheritance. Perhaps he was the one who killed her?"

Lilly briefly closed her eyes and hoped Bonnie would make an appearance soon. Things were getting out of hand in here.

* * *

"SUSANNA, REALLY! I wouldn't have put you down as a gossip," Lady Gresham said.

"And you'd be correct, Meredith," Susanna replied, unperturbed by the older woman's tone. "But surely it's natural to want to discuss the unexplained death of someone you knew? It's a form of comfort and sharing a problem rather than bottling it up and worrying about it alone. Besides, this is how Lilly works. Isn't that right, Lilly? Talking to people and gathering together what they say to see what doesn't add up. She's solved a number of cases in our town over the last year or so. You never know, but discussing it could help us provide pertinent information to Bonnie in order for her to find the culprit."

Lilly gritted her teeth but kept her mouth shut. She hated being put on the spot like this, but Susanna did have a valid point. It was the way she had worked on the previous cases and providing nothing was discussed beyond this room she saw no harm in collating the information all these women knew to see if anything was relevant. She said as much to the others.

"Well, I wasn't going to say anything now she's dead, but..." Mrs Davenport said.

"What do you know?" Meredith asked her, her voice filled with unsurprising skepticism. Hopefully, Mrs Davenport wasn't just seeking attention and had something useful to impart, rather than her usual salacious gossip.

"I overheard some of the other artists talking about Annabelle this morning. They were terribly rude about her work. Calling it contrived nonsense and particularly bad art that they wouldn't give house room. Apparently, they said she

45

was a talented nobody who used her family's money to buy acceptance and credibility."

"What complete and utter nonsense," Meredith spat. "Art was Abigail's life and her true passion. She was incredibly talented and her work was superb."

"I agree," Lilly said. "These other artists were simply jealous and probably saw her as a threat. Who was it you heard, Mrs Davenport?"

"I don't know. I was in the cloakroom, hanging up my coat, and they were on the other side of the partition. I would possibly recognise a voice if I heard it, but I wouldn't know what they looked like."

Lilly wondered if anyone in that group was jealous enough to commit murder? Admittedly, the prizes were excellent but surely not worth enough to go to that extreme?

"I admit to being wholly uneducated when it comes to the art world," Lilly said. "Was Annabelle well known? Had she won awards or achieved recognition nationally for her work?"

"National and international," Meredith confirmed. "She's won numerous awards and held solo exhibitions in various capitals around the world, including our own. But she was only ever an amateur. That isn't a judgement about her work, by the way. But she wasn't in the business of making money from her art. That's the difference between a professional and an amateur. Professional is more the description of the work as a business as opposed to the artist."

"I understand. In that case, it's no wonder the others saw her as a threat."

"It's such a shame," Mrs Davenport said. "She was such a lovely, selfless woman."

"Nobody's perfect," Susanna said with feeling.

Lilly was about to ask her what she meant when they were interrupted by Bonnie.

"Lilly, could you come out here please? I'd like to speak with you."

Lilly's heart thumped. She didn't like Bonnie's tone at all.

Chapter Six

LILLY WAS FEELING the heat rise in her face as she followed Bonnie from the room. The inflection in her voice had not been that of a friend but of a detective on a serious case about to interrogate a suspect.

"How can I help, Bonnie?"

Bonnie opened a nearby door and, checking it was vacant, indicated Lilly should enter. She closed the door firmly, then peering briefly out of the window, pulled the curtains closed and turned to face her.

It was obvious to Lilly that something was wrong, but she couldn't for the life of her work out what it was.

"Is there something you want to tell me?" Bonnie said.

Lilly didn't know what she was getting at. She had no secrets from Bonnie. She shook her head.

"No. Not that I can think of."

"Are you sure?"

"Yes, of course I am. Bonnie, what's going on?"

"I've just finished speaking with Mable Standish. She had some interesting things to say."

"Okay. Like what?"

"You had lunch the other day with the judges and you and she stayed behind to discuss the catering for this event, yes?"

"Yes. But what has that got to do with what's happened to Annabelle?"

"She informed me you were jealous of Annabelle's new tea shop and extremely worried about how badly it would affect your business."

Lilly's stomach clenched. Now she understood what this was about. Lilly couldn't believe Mable had told Bonnie what she'd said. She'd told the woman in confidence. Well, at least now she knew where she stood. No doubt idle tongues were at that very moment wagging in the green room, but she was more aggrieved at the way Bonnie was questioning her. She knew Bonnie needed to explore all avenues, but her tone was accusatory and it was making Lilly angry. She took a seat, crossed her legs, and folded her arms. Glaring at her friend defiantly.

"Yes, all right. I admit I was a bit jealous, and worried about my own business. Wouldn't you be? But not enough to kill her, Bonnie. How can you think such a thing? How long have we known one another?"

Bonnie sat opposite and leaned on the table.

"I'm sorry, Lilly, but right now you're my main suspect."

"Oh, for god's sake, Bonnie. I can't believe you just said that. It's ridiculous. I didn't kill Annabelle Haines and quite frankly, I'm both insulted and pretty upset that you'd think I did. Why would you even suggest such a thing?"

Bonnie raised her hands placatingly and leaned back.

"I know you didn't, Lilly."

"What? Well, what's this all about then?"

Bonnie removed her phone from her knee and put it on the table. Tapping the screen to stop the recording. Lilly stared at the phone, then at her friend.

"You recorded our conversation?"

"I'm really sorry, Lilly. Truly I am, but Annabelle Haines was a big deal in this town. She came from a wealthy background and both she and her family have done a lot for Plumpton Mallet. She moved in all the right circles and because of her international reputation as an artist, was one of our most well known residents. Consequently, it's not only my boss who wants immediate answers, but my boss's boss."

Lilly sat back and waited for Bonnie to continue. She didn't trust herself to speak in case she said something she would regret. She was absolutely livid.

"The thing is, Lilly, you and I are friends and I've allowed you to assist in a lot of serious and high-profile cases. The big chief has questioned my decision to let you become involved when you've usually been the one to discover the victim. He's now asking awkward questions and intimating subterfuge on your behalf."

"You mean he thinks I've been working with the criminals for some utterly unknown and bizarre reason, then insinuating myself into the case to solve it and make myself look good?"

"That's it exactly."

"Does he think I have some sort of backwards Munchausens or something?"

"Isn't that where the Oompa Loompa's lived?" Bonnie said with a straight face but a definite twinkle in her eye.

Lilly felt a bubble of mirth start somewhere in her chest.

"Oh no, wait," Bonnie said. "I'm wrong. It's the little country they went to in Chitty Chitty Bang Bang to save Granddad, right?"

The bubble burst and Lilly laughed. It was what Bonnie was hoping for.

"I'm sorry, Lilly. I had to play it the way I did in order to get a wholly natural reaction from you on record. Believe me, after this, no one is going to believe you're involved."

"Of course I'm not involved! So you were attempting to prove my innocence while treating me like the worst of criminals?" Bonnie nodded a little sheepishly. "The boss of your boss is a fool in that case."

"Well, he was fast-tracked because of his name not due to his little grey cells, as Poirot would say. I don't think he's ever walked the beat in his life."

"So what now?" Lilly asked.

"Now, I will take your statement. And for goodness' sake, don't mention how jealous you are of Annabelle's shop. A little envious is fine, that's understandable. But nothing more. You were found with the body, Lilly, and there are several witnesses. Some of whom are no doubt thinking the worst. And others who were recording you on their phones. We've managed to confiscate all of those so they won't see the light of day, by the way. But it's not stopping the whispers and the gossip. We both know you're innocent, but that means the real killer is still wandering about out there. We need to find them quickly. So tell me your movements today, starting from when you walked through the door."

Lilly took a deep breath. She knew Bonnie wanted to be able to prove she was not alone at any time, or if she was that she didn't have time to murder Annabelle Haines.

* * *

L ILLY GAVE BONNIE a step-by-step account, starting with briefly stopping to see Stacey and Abigail and the buffet they'd put together for the event. She then moved onto entering the green room and convening with her fellow judges.

"What did you talk about?" Bonnie asked.

"About the previous competitions. The prizes and how they would be shared between the winners. I obviously had questions about how it all worked, with it being my first stint as a judge. They explained all of that and Susanna asked what I was expecting to see in a winning entry. Then Archie arrived."

"Archie?" Bonnie said, raising an eyebrow. "What did he want?"

"He said he came to interview us for the paper, which he did. But he actually had popped by to see me and wish me luck. He'd hoped to catch me before I went into the meeting, but was late. He gave all his notes to the junior who actually will be writing the article."

Bonnie shook her head and gave a wry a smile.

"Go on."

"After he left, it was time for us to go to the exhibition space. The names of the artists had already been covered up, so we would be judging blind. Lady Gresham lead us around, starting with the youngest age group and moving through to the oldest. She does it every year, apparently. She's the biggest sponsor of the event. The public had already been asked to vacate the space and move to the bar and buffet, so we had the place to ourselves."

Lilly briefly told Bonnie about the paintings, Mrs Davenport's desire to impress, and Lady Gresham's extensive knowledge of art.

"Once we'd finished, Mable suggested we take a short break before reconvening in the green room to discuss the winners. I wanted to take another quick circuit around the room just to double check who I thought should win each individual category and the competition overall. I made one small change."

Bonnie frowned.

"How long did that take?"

"About fifteen minutes. I was on my way back to the other judges when I found Annabelle. I ran over to see if there was anything I could do. I checked for a pulse but didn't find one. The rest, you know."

"Okay." Bonnie said. "For the majority of the time you're with someone else, but that fifteen minutes you were wandering around the exhibition space alone is problematic, Lilly. You had more than enough time to leave, kill Annabelle, then return to the green room or elsewhere."

Lilly leaned on the table and put her head in her hands, nodding.

"I know," came her muffled reply.

She was becoming aware that no matter whether Bonnie believed her or not, it could easily be made to fit that she had both motive and opportunity to commit the murder. She got up and began to pace. She couldn't sit still when she was feeling so agitated. And she thought better when she was moving.

"Bonnie, I know I didn't kill Annabelle, no matter what it looks like. But I have to find out who did in order to prove my innocence."

Bonnie stood as well.

"Wait, a minute! Didn't you just hear me say how much trouble we're in with my superiors because I've let you help before? I could be up for a disciplinary if I let you start snooping around this time. You are still a suspect, Lilly."

"Then we'll have to be careful so they don't know."

"Lilly!"

"No, I don't care, Bonnie. I am not going to sit around with a Sword of Damocles hang over my head. Not knowing if I'm about to be accused and arrested for a murder I didn't commit. You obviously don't have any other leads, which tells me you need help. Who better to help than the person who has to clear her name?"

Bonnie folded her arms, looked at the floor, and started her own pacing. Lilly remained quiet, watching. Every so often, Bonnie would kick the leg of the table or a chair in frustration. Eventually, she looked at her friend.

"All right. But absolutely no one must know. I mean it, Lilly. No one. We keep this quiet and you report anything you hear or see to me directly. And not in public. Face-to-face meetings at your house or mine and after work hours. The tea shop or the cafe at a push depending on how long the investigation takes. God forbid it drags on that long, but you're right, I have no other leads at the moment. Mobile phone calls only if it's urgent. And no texts or emails. Use Archie as a go between to get word to me, or to pass on info. As the local crime reporter, he and I are in constant touch anyway, so it won't look suspicious."

"I can't believe it's come to this," Lilly said. "But thank you. Both for letting me help and for believing me. So did you find anything in the room Annabelle was found?"

Bonnie smirked.

"Come on. I'll show you. Let me just make sure the way is clear."

* * *

THERE WAS A UNIFORMED OFFICER standing guard out-side the room, but Annabelle's body had been removed and transported to the morgue for the Post Mortem.

They both entered and after telling her officer they weren't to be disturbed, Bonnie shut the door.

"Can you trust him?" Lilly asked, indicating to the officer outside.

"Yes. He won't say anything. He admires the current top brass as much as I do."

For a short moment neither of them moved, just absorbed the scene before them. There was a small seating area in one corner and diagonally opposite a long table covered with a paint splattered oilskin cloth. By the windows, two easels stood side-by-side next to a table littered with brushes, bottles and rags. In the centre was a cleared space the size of a stan-dard canvas.

To the side of the table was another canvas, blank except

for a daub of green paint in the bottom corner which looked like a cross.

"What exactly is this room?" Lilly asked Bonnie.

"According to Mable, it's where the artists can add finishing touches to their work if they need to, prior to exhibiting it."

Lilly approached the single canvas.

"Do you know who this belonged to?"

"No. But, for your ears only, Annabelle's hand was covered in green paint. It looked as though she was about to start another piece of work when she was interrupted by the killer."

"Yes, she was a prolific painter. She needed to create as much as she needed to breathe, by all accounts."

She turned and looked back at the room.

"What are we looking for, Bonnie?"

"Clues of some sort. You should know that being our resident sleuth."

"A moniker I don't want to have today. Honestly, I never in a million years thought my day would end up like this when I walked in this morning. I was really looking forward to being a judge. Now I'm facing the prospect of being accused of murder."

Lilly wished desperately that she could talk to Archie. He was her sounding board, her main source of support and comfort.

"We'll find them, Lilly."

"We have to, Bonnie."

She started searching on the left-hand side of the room furthest away from where she'd found Annabelle and the drying pool of blood which, apart from her work, was the only thing that remained of such a vibrant life.

She found an artist's smock liberally splattered in purple and pink paint. She hung it back on the hook and moved on. She searched behind a stack of paint cans but found nothing. Under the table, she found some scraps of paper and picked them up. But again, they were just wrappers you'd find on children's crayons. She put them back. Nowhere did she find green paint.

She checked behind the potted ferns and lifted a small rug when she spied a bump. But it was a stray brush with clean bristles. Similarly, the small bowl of fruit on a side table yielded no clues. The windows were closed and locked, but behind the easels was a small table covered in tubes of oil, watercolour, and acrylic paints. Large jam jars full of murky liquid housed brushes in the midst of being cleaned.

She moved to the large table and lifted the cloth. Underneath was a beautiful oak table. No wonder there was a waterproof cloth on it.

Pushed against a side wall was a small desk. Lilly opened a drawer, but apart from a layer of dust and cobwebs, it was empty. In the other drawer, she found a child's drawing stuffed right at the back. It had probably been there for years with no one the wiser. She returned it and moved to the adjacent waste bin. She carefully moved aside the empty paint tubes and discarded brushes, but found nothing of interest.

As she turned, her foot caught something trapped behind the desk. It was a plug. Pulling on the flex revealed a hairdryer. It must have fallen from the desk and become trapped behind.

"Bonnie, I've found a hairdryer. Do you think it's important?"

Bonnie wandered over and took a look.

"Blimey, it weighs a ton. I think my mum had this model in the seventies."

"Yes, it looks vintage," Lilly said.

"It's also badly cracked. Possibly from when it fell off the desk. But this room is also used for the dramatics society. It could belong to them. Why would an artist need a hairdryer?"

"I'm not sure," Lilly replied. "Maybe they used it to dry the paint if they'd done some touch ups?"

"Good thinking. That's more than possible."

Bonnie carefully turned the hairdryer over to inspect the other side.

"Wait, what's this?"

Lilly peered at the splot.

"Red paint?"

"Or blood," Bonnie replied. "I can't tell the difference now it's almost dry. I'll need to have it analysed."

"Did you find anything on your side?"

"Paint brushes and used rags. Nothing you wouldn't expect from an impromptu art studio. We've done all we can in here, Lilly. You go back to the green room and remember we are not working together. I'll let you know what I find out and you can do the same. But for now, keep a low profile. Or as Archie would put it, eyes peeled and mouth shut."

Chapter Seven

LILLY TURNED in the opposite direction from Bonnie and with a heavy heart and a lot of anxiety, began her return journey to her fellow judges. She was still smarting from the fact that Mable had quite happily blurted out how Lilly felt about the new tea shop to Bonnie. The woman probably thought she was doing the right thing. However, Lilly had learned her lesson and wouldn't tell Mable anything in confidence again.

While she was reluctantly trudging back to the green room, she remembered the previous conversation. There were a couple of instances which mentioned Annabelle in a less than favourable light. She should have told Bonnie, but with the shock of being the main suspect and facing arrest, it had completely slipped her mind. At least it was somewhere she could start her own investigation.

Turning a corner, she nearly bumped into two older teenagers. Eighteen or nineteen, Lilly thought. She wondered why they were wandering around this area.

"Oops, sorry," she said. "Are you lost?"

They shook their heads.

"I'm one of the artists," the youth said. "My name is Eddie, and this is my sister Elisa."

"I'm Lilly." It was on the tip of her tongue to mention she was a judge, but thought better of it. She didn't know what the protocol was prior to the winners being announced. Instead, she opted for, "So, which entry is yours?"

"I'm in the first age group. I did a still life."

"The hand carved bowl with fruit?" Lilly asked. She probably shouldn't be having this conversation, but she'd just remembered what Mrs Davenport had said about overhearing a group of artists gossiping about Annabelle. Maybe he had some information.

The boy nodded.

"I don't think my chances are very good now, though. I didn't see many other still lifes in the exhibition."

"No, but yours stood out for that very reason. It was very good. You're a very accomplished artist for someone so young. Do you take lessons?"

"Actually, I'm nearly twenty," he said. Still young compared to me, Lilly thought. "I used to have a teacher, but I wanted to see what I could do on my own. My Gran wanted me to carry on but..." the boy tailed off, swallowing hard and looking down at the carpet.

"She was a brilliant artist," his sister said, beginning to cry.

"Are you all right?" Lilly asked.

The girl shook her head.

"Our Gran died today."

Lilly's heart sank to the pit of her stomach.

"You must be Annabelle's grandchildren?" she said gently. "I am so sorry."

Lilly was now stuck. How on earth was she supposed to question these two when they were not just young, but grieving? Meredith had mentioned the grandchildren had been taken out of Annabelle's will, but Lilly had been expecting them to be older. They were little more than kids. Surely they couldn't be responsible for her death? On the other hand, she needed some information to find the real killer or she could find herself arrested.

"Thank you," Elisa said, wiping her eyes and nose on her sleeve. "I can't believe she's dead."

Eddie put his arm around his sister's shoulders.

"Were you close?"

"Yes. It was her art that inspired me to try," Eddie said.

"We loved visiting her and seeing her new work. She was such good fun. We'll really miss her."

This wasn't the response Lilly had been expecting. If there had been a family fall out, which the changing of the will seemed to indicate, she'd have expected, at the very least, anger or resentment. There was nothing but genuine love here.

"I visited her new tea shop the other day. The murals and her framed pictures were beautiful. She was very talented."

"We haven't visited there yet," Eddie said. "Now I don't suppose we will."

"Oh?" Lilly said. "I would have thought the first people she'd share it with would be family. You didn't have a falling out, did you?"

It was clumsy, but the best Lilly could think to say on the spur of the moment.

"No," Eddie said. "Why would ask that?" he was beginning to sound angry. "We've just lost our Gran. Hey, wait a minute. Did you say your name was Lilly? Aren't you the one who owns the tea shop in town?"

"You found her, didn't you?" Elisa said, beginning to sound as annoyed as her brother. "Why are you still walking around questioning us? The police should have arrested you."

"You're right, I do have tea shop in town and I did find your Gran, but I was trying to help her."

"I don't believe you," Eddie spat out. "You were jealous that her business would be better than yours. I bet you wanted her dead."

"Of course I didn't. I would never hurt Annabelle."

"We'll see what the police have to say. You shouldn't be allowed to walk around free. Come on Elisa."

He grabbed his sister's arm and the two of them hurried back to the exhibition.

Lilly stared after them, absolutely dumbstruck. This time, she had pushed her luck too far.

* * *

IT WAS A VERY SUBDUED and distraught Lilly who continued through the hall. She desperately wanted to talk to a friend. Hear a familiar voice of someone on her side. Someone who had unshakable faith in her innocence. She pulled out her phone and called Archie. It went straight to voice mail. Which upset Lilly more than it should have done. No doubt with a real crime to investigate, he was gathering all the information he could. But she was close to tears. She tried Stacey, but she didn't answer either.

She leaned against the wall, trying to pull herself together. Meredith had mentioned the will, and that surely indicated a family argument of some kind? Annabelle wouldn't have written out her grandchildren unless something terrible had happened. But why in that case had Eddie and Elisa denied any sort of falling out? Going so far as to act shocked that she would even ask the question. From what they said, their relationship with their Gran was excellent. They loved her. But Lilly also felt Eddie had been hiding something. Or at least not telling the whole truth. He was too quick to anger, too defensive. In fact, they both were. But did it mean anything in terms of the murder?

Then there was the nasty conversation about Annabelle that Mrs Davenport had overheard. Surely her own grandson wouldn't have been one of the artists involved? He was an excellent artist in his own right, although, of course, Annabelle was better. But that came with age and years of practice and experience. No doubt in a few years'ran's talent and reputation be a strong enough motive for him to have killed her? If the case for the will was proved,ain, but it was extremely unlikely he'd be amenable to any more of her questions after his parting shot.

She sighed and moved on. Deciding to drop by the kitchen first to see Stacey and Abigail.

She pushed open the door expecting to see her friends, but the room was empty. There were trays of food waiting to go to the buffet table and teapots warming on the side, but no sign of anyone. Lilly was starting to get concerned when Stacey appeared.

"There you are," she said. "I tried calling you. Where have you been?"

"We've been trying to keep up with feeding everyone. The police moved everyone into the buffet room after what happened. Are you all right, Lilly? You don't look well."

"I'm fine. Just a bit stressed, if I'm honest."

"Is it true you were the one who found Annabelle?"

"Yes, unfortunately. I'm all right, Stacey, don't worry. It's not the first time I've fallen over a corpse," she replied, trying to keep it light. She was aware she'd promised Bonnie not to breathe a word about them working to clear her name.

"Are you investigating?"

"Maybe a little, but not much. I'm trying to keep out of Bonnie's way. If she needs me to help, then I'm sure she'll ask."

"She better," Stacey said forcefully. "There's a real nasty rumour going round, Lilly. I'm not sure I should tell you, but I guess you'll hear soon enough and it will be better coming from me. They are saying you killed Annabelle. I've told anyone who'll listen it's not true and so far I've managed to squash the gossip. But you know what this town's like."

"Thank you, Stacey. I appreciate it. I was afraid that might happen."

"That's why Abigail wanted to go out and serve customers. She wanted to talk positively about you and stop the rumours."

"It was a good idea," Lilly said. "And if it's working, then I should distance myself from you both while we're here. I don't want the tea shop or the cafe to be tarnished with what's happened. Even though it's all lies."

Stacey nodded, a look of concern on her face.

"Okay. But just so you know, me, Abigail and the rest of the team know you are innocent. If there's anything we can do to help, just let me know." Her phone buzzed, and she saw a text from Abigail. "I need to take some more food out to the buffet. Give me a shout if you need anything, Lilly. We're all behind you."

Lilly swallowed the lump in her throat as Stacey, after giving her a fierce hug, left with a tray of delectables for the hungry crowd. Thank goodness she had her friends to support her.

As she left the kitchen, her mind to the gossip currently circulating the crowds. It spread so fast in a place like Plumpton Mallet. She also wondered if Eddie was adding fuel to an already out-of-control fire. It was worrying her, and she hoped Bonnie wasn't giving into pressure. There was only so much she could do before her superiors demanded action. It was exhausting, and she chided herself for not getting a cup of tea. She really could have done with a calming and energy boosting drink. But she'd just have to do without for the moment and hope the adrenaline kept pumping through her veins, giving her the stamina she needed to get through it all.

Outside the green room, she took a breath. She was nervous. She had no idea what she was about to face inside or how they would react to her. She was fully expecting insults and accusations. Or at the very least, hard questions. Perhaps none of them would talk to her at all. Choosing to ignore her completely. She didn't know which would be worse.

"But if you don't open the door, you'll never know," she said to herself.

She gripped the handle and pushed. She stopped in the entryway. This wasn't what she had expected at all.

Chapter Eight

THE ROOM WAS COMPLETELY EMPTY. The notepads and pens were still on the table, open, as though all the judges had decided to leave en masse while still in the middle of their deliberations. She closed the door and approached the table, seeing the list Lady Gresham had made.

She sat down and waited. Surely they'd return soon? She took the opportunity to prepare some notes about her investigation. Putting her jumbled thoughts in order. When she'd finished, she tore the page out of the pad and, folding it, put it in her pocket. She didn't want anyone knowing she was snooping into Annabelle's death.

Moving to the tea table, she found a still warm pot of tea and poured herself a cup, leaning against the table while she sipped.

Fifteen minutes later, with none of the other judges having made an appearance, she decided to go in search of them. Perhaps they'd already made their decisions and were enjoying the buffet or had gone outside to stretch their legs until the time came to announce the winners.

She returned to the hall and went in the opposite direction. As she turned the corner, she almost bumped into Mrs Davenport.

"Oh, Lilly!" the woman said, grasping Lilly's hand. "How are you? Goodness, what a dreadful set of circumstances. You must be beside yourself?"

"I'm fine, Mrs Davenport. Thank you. Where is everyone? I've just been waiting in the green room but no one is there."

"No. We decided to get some fresh air. I paid a visit to the powder room on the way and when I came out, they'd gone. I can't seem to find anyone either."

Lilly felt a pang of sympathy for the woman. She looked so sad and dejected. The others had obviously deliberately ditched her at the first opportunity. It was true, Mrs Davenport was an incorrigible gossip with a tendency to be tactless, but Lilly felt sure she knew why the others had left without her. She must be feeling terrible. And her first question was how Lilly was. Lilly couldn't help but feel mean by her own uncharitable thoughts. The woman was obviously lonely and trying to make friends the best way she knew how. She swore to herself that she'd do better in the future.

"Shall we go outside and try to find them?" Lilly suggested.

"Oh yes. That's a good idea. I'd be happy to have the company."

"Well, if we can't see them, we could have a coffee at The End of the Line cafe, across the road. My treat."

"Really? Oh, that would be lovely. Thank you, Lilly."

They managed to leave unseen and outside, crossed over

the road to admire the new floral planters that stretched from one end of the train station plaza to the other. They'd been built from large sandstone blocks from the local quarry, topped with shaped coping stones and stocked with a stunning array of seasonal flowers by local volunteers.

After a few minutes where Mrs Davenport explained what each flower was, and the best environment in which to make them thrive, they moved to a secluded table outside the coffee shop. Over steaming, frothy mugs of cappuccino, Lilly began asking her companion some questions.

"Have you remembered anything else about the conversation you overheard regarding Annabelle?"

"Not really. The man who started it was just very rude about her."

"It was a man? Could you gauge how old?"

"I would hazard a guess at middle age. It's difficult to tell when you can't see the person, isn't it? Certainly not young. In fact, the other couple of voices I heard were of similar age. Another male and one female."

So it was unlikely to be Annabelle's grandson Eddie in the group. Lilly thought to herself. Because regardless of whether he thought nearly twenty was old, he still sounded like a youth. She had wondered. In fact, if she was honest, she had hoped he would be. Being written out of your grandmother's will would certainly be a motive for murder. But annoyingly, it looked as though she was no further forward.

"They were all very pretentious and showy, if you get my drift?" Mrs Davenport continued.

"And you're sure you didn't see anything that could identify them?"

"Oh dear. I do know how important this is, Lilly, but it was first thing this morning. Hours ago and so much has happened since then. I've been wracking my brains since you found poor Annabelle and the only extra thing I remember is the cravat. Although I can't see what use that would be."

"Cravat?" Lilly asked.

"Yes. It was when they were leaving the cloak room. I came around the corner as a man was just exiting. The others had gone, and he pulled a canary yellow cravat from his pocket then disappeared."

Now that is a clue I can follow, Lilly thought as a plan began to formulate in her mind.

* * *

LILLY LEANED OVER the table and dropped her voice to barely more than a whisper.

"Mrs Davenport. I have a plan. But I need your help."

The woman did likewise, mirroring Lilly's movement. She had a bright, shining spark in her eye and positively vibrated with excitement.

"Are you sleuthing, Lilly?"

"I'm not supposed to be, and it's only to get an answer to one question. But you must keep quiet about it, Mrs Davenport, or I could get into serious trouble."

Mrs Davenport mimed locking her lips and throwing away the key.

"I shan't say a word. I promise. Now, I shall happily be Watson to your Sherlock. What did you have in mind?"

Lilly laid out her plans as succinctly as possible. Explaining her reasons fully and her coffee companion listened carefully. When Lilly got to the part, she needed help with Mrs Davenport nodded and smiled purposely.

"I know just the place, Lilly. Follow me. It's best if we go in the back door. That way we won't be seen and it leads to the room we need."

On their way back to the venue. Lilly took one more glance around the outside. There was no sign of the other judges. She wondered where they had all gone?

"Better keep your head down, Lilly," Mrs Davenport whispered. "I can see your colleagues in the kitchen."

They moved cautiously, keeping to the shadows under the perimeter wall, but Abigail and Stacey were too busy to notice them. At the entrance, they sneaked into the hall and Mrs Davenport indicated a door.

"It leads downstairs," she whispered. "So be careful of your footing."

The light was already on when they descended into the hallway below. Mrs Davenport bustled off and Lilly followed. After a few minutes they reached a door with a sign proclaiming it to be for the Principal.

"Where on earth are we?" Lilly asked.

"Underneath the building. At the back of the stage. This is where the Amateur Dramatics Society gets ready for the shows. I'm a member of the wardrobe department," Mrs Davenport told her with a huge grin. "Now, you wait in here and I'll go and find the key we need. I won't be long."

The room was small, not much larger than a broom cupboard, but with some clever design it had been kitted out with all the accoutrements a lead actor would need. A chair and dressing table with the vanity mirror surrounded by Hollywood style bulbs. A free standing rail for the costumes with a shoe rack beneath. A large decoupaged screen in the far corner for making costume changes in privacy and an old-fashioned serving trolley on wheels, where a kettle stood alongside an empty vase. On the shelf below was an empty ice bucket in readiness for a bottle of champagne to celebrate either opening night or the end of the run.

The door opened.

"PssstPst. Lilly, I've got the key," Mrs Davenport said. "Come on."

Further down the hall, she unlocked a door and switched on a light. They both entered and Lilly looked around her in amazement.

Racks upon racks of costumes from different eras filled the space. From pirates to flamingos, spacemen to old maids, there was everything imaginable.

Lilly swept her hand down a turquoise feather boa and lifted a hat with a playing card tucked in the rim.

"I don't think that will quite work, Lilly," Mrs Davenport said in all seriousness.

Lilly laughed.

"No. Gangster comedy a la Bugsy Malone will definitely defeat the purpose. So where are the more appropriate disguises?"

"Just down here. We've staged many a contemporary production, but it doesn't take much to change your look. A wig and a pair of glasses should do the trick. Perhaps a long coat to cover our clothes."

They spent several minutes searching for something suitable, then began to don their outfits.

Lilly had opted for a shoulder length dark ginger wig to cover her own dark hair. A pair of large tortoiseshell glasses and a long belted mackintosh. Cream coloured and lightweight, which wouldn't look out of place at this time of year.

"Good heavens," exclaimed Mrs Davenport. "I really wouldn't have known it was you, Lilly. But I think a couple of additions and it will be perfect."

She moved to a table and found a pair of large gold clip-on earrings in the shape of knots, and another lipstick, this time in a deep burgundy. A colour Lilly had never worn in her life. She glanced in the mirror and found she hardly recognised herself.

"You look completely different as well, Mrs Davenport. If you don't mind me saying so, it takes years off you."

The elderly woman had chosen a black wig cut in a severe bob which perfectly covered her short, nearly white hair. Cats eye shaped glasses in purple, replete with silver chain and a slash of red lipstick completed the look. Over her own clothes, she wore a long green velvet cloak and in her hand carried a floral decorated walking stick. Around her neck were several large chains of multi-coloured beads.

"Does it really? How wonderful! Perhaps I'm long overdue a makeover. I say, it's rather exciting, isn't it? Right then, my dear. Let's get this show on the road, shall we? Break a leg!"

* * *

THE KITCHEN WAS EMPTY as the two of them retraced their footsteps through the backyard and down the side of the building to the front. Outside the venue's main entrance, they mounted the steps and ventured into the main event hall, sliding effortlessly to join the milling crowd. They were on the lookout for a canary yellow cravat.

Lilly hoped he wasn't in the buffet room. While her current partner in crime had assured her that even her nearest and dearest wouldn't recognise her, she wasn't wholly convinced. The last thing she needed was for either Abigail or Stacey to realise who she was. Or worse, one of the other judges. Her stomach clenched, and she bowed her head, causing the hair of the wig to cover most of her face. Her neck was in danger of seizing up, but at least no one would know who she was.

They began a circuit on the outskirts of the room, keeping to the shadows, and it wasn't long before Lilly felt a tug on her sleeve. Mrs Davenport indicated a group of people just up ahead. In the centre was a man wearing a yellow cravat. They moved closer to hear the conversation.

"What is your rationale for its usage, Mr Jones?" one woman asked.

"Crayon is not the most common of mediums, but believe me, it is the future. It's inventive, experimental and innovative. I have a more The Avant-Garde approach compared to the other entries, which if I'm honest are all terribly clichéd. I'm sure you all agree? I mean, if you've seen one still life in oil, you've seen them all," he said airily. "No, the art world needs shaking up. We need to break new ground and produce cutting-edge and contemporary work. Work that makes people question their very existence and which elicits a visceral response. Tapping the unconscious mind like the surrealists once did. And that, my dear audience, is my intent. It's not about the accolades or the cold hard cash. No, it's about the art and only the art. As long as I have my materials and a small place to work with some natural light and preferably a roof," he smiled modestly, "that's enough for me."

Lilly rolled her eyes. It all sounded like pretentious nonsense to her. This man obviously felt that suffering for your art was the mark of the true artist. Anything else was just imitation. He was the sort of person who would relish living in a damp garret in Paris. A starving artist existing hand to mouth in one room. Sleeping on a cot and wearing rags.

"I don't know, Travis," the man next to him said. "I don't think this town in ready for a crayon art revolution."

"I'm not talking about this, no offense, rather parochial competition. I'm talking about the world stage."

So the man in the yellow canary cravat was called Travis Jones. He must also be the owner of the odd, rather childish and out-of-place entry Mrs Davenport had liked during the judge's viewing.

They'd found what they had come for, so Lilly was about to suggest to Mrs Davenport that they leave rather than risk being recognised, when someone in the group mentioned Annabelle.

"What happened to Annabelle was shocking. Monstrous! Such a cruel loss to the world of art," Travis said, taking a blue and white spotted handkerchief from his waistcoat pocket and wiping his eyes.

Lilly was standing to his side and back slightly, deliberately out of his field of vision, but she could see those tears were real. She was a little surprised by his immediate response. Considering he had supposedly been bad-mouthing Annabelle earlier, he certainly seemed sincere in his sorrow now. Perhaps Mrs

Davenport had got the wrong end of the stick? She saw a man exit the cloakroom and pull a yellow cravat from his pocket. But it didn't mean he was part of the conversation she had overheard. He could simply have been there at the time but not part of it, like Mrs Davenport herself was. It was looking as though all this dressing up and infiltrating the audience had been a complete waste of time. Lilly was irked as the one true lead she had evaporated before her eyes.

"She really was the matriarch of our artist community," Travis continued. "Such a selfless soul who was always happy to lend a hand to those who needed it most. Nothing was too much trouble for her. I, for one, shall miss her dreadfully." He lifted his teacup and saucer from a nearby table and raised it. "A toast to Annabelle. I hope you're painting with the angels."

Lilly was convinced Travis genuinely did miss Annabelle. Mrs Davenport must have heard someone else. This particular clue was a dead end, and it was time they left.

"We need to go," she whispered in the other woman's ear.

"Already? But he's such an eloquent speaker." She gave a wistful sigh. "I could listen to him all day."

"And we'll get in trouble if he recognises us," Lilly hissed.

At the mention of trouble, Mrs Davenport reared back. She'd obviously forgotten the reason they were there. She turned but was in too much of a hurry and tripped over her own feet. She fell backwards. Right into the arms of Travis Jones.

Chapter Nine

LILLY GASPED as Travis swooped in and caught Mrs Davenport before she hit the floor. Pretentious or not, his reflexes were excellent.

"Goodness, that was close," Mrs Davenport said, nudging her skewed glasses back onto her nose. Luckily, her wig hadn't moved an inch. "I practically saw my life flash before my eyes. Thank you, young man. You saved my dignity and, most likely, a broken hip."

"You're most welcome," Travis Jones said. "I'm always happy to help a damsel in distress. You obviously know me, but I don't think I've had the pleasure?"

"Just think of me as your number one fan," she replied coquettishly.

Lilly stood with her mouth gaping as Mrs Davenport flirted shamelessly with the artist. But at least she wasn't blowing their cover. Lilly was stunned at the older woman's transformation. There was nothing left of the Mrs Davenport, she knew. Even her accent had taken on a West Country burr.

"Now, perhaps you'd be good enough to escort me to the powder room? I'm still a little shaky."

"I'd be delighted."

The two of them meandered their way through the crowd arm-in-arm with Lilly close behind them.

"Come along, dear," Mrs Davenport said over her shoulder to Lilly. "My niece," she explained to Travis. "She's a quiet child, but was good enough to bring me to the event today. Of course, it was your art I was hoping to see. Tell me more about the medium you use. I find it fascinating."

Lilly shook her head in wonderment. Forget being tucked away out of sight in the wardrobe department. She firmly believed Mrs Davenport belonged on the stage.

As they neared the ladies' room, Travis Jones stopped and suggested he wait. Mrs Davenport thumped him playfully on his arm.

"Silly boy. That was just an excuse to get you alone. There's a lovely secluded seating area just down here. I suggest we sit awhile. I believe your art is for sale, is it not?"

Shortly after they'd sat down, while Mrs Davenport expertly pandered to the artist's ego, not to mention his wallet, Stacey arrived with a tea tray and a selection of food from the buffet. She performed an exaggerated double-take at Lilly, her eyes widening and her mouth falling open. Lilly, stifling a laugh with great difficulty, gave an almost imperceptible shake of head and Stacey, after an equally shocked glance at Mrs Davenport, left them. A couple of minutes later, Abigail turned up with a pot of boiling water to refresh the tea that hadn't even been poured yet. She eyed Lilly with a raised eyebrow and, likewise, her partner in crime before moving away, a smirk on her lips.

Lilly sighed. So much for the disguise. She'd never hear the end of this. She poured three cups of tea while listening to the conversation next to her. Hopefully she'd hear something of use meaning the rigmarole of dressing up hadn't all been for nothing.

* * *

"I ABSOLUTELY ADORE your competition entry, Travis. Such a vibrant and clever use of colour."

"I can tell you appreciate great art when you see it," Travis replied.

"Oh, I do. Although it's purely intuitive. A matter of knowing what I like and what I don't. It's the work that speaks to me. I've had no formal training as it were."

"Neither have I, my dear lady. I'm purely self-taught."

"You do surprise me. You were obviously born with a great deal of natural talent."

Lilly just about managed not to choke on her tea.

"I do wish everyone could see what you do. Perhaps then I'd be recognised for the true artist I am," Travis said.

"Doesn't everyone see your flair for genius?"

"Sadly not. I was recently called a talentless oaf!"

"How appalling. Who on earth said that?"

Travis waved his hand.

"I don't want to speak ill of the dead."

"You don't mean Annabelle Haines, do you?" Mrs Davenport asked, and Lilly almost applauded.

"Why yes. Did you know her?"

"No, but considering what has just happened, I assumed that's who you meant. Why was she so rude to you?"

"Well, she's opening, or rather was opening, a new gallery and tea shop on the outskirts of town and was intending to showcase pieces from local artists. Naturally, I spoke with her about my work. It would have been an excellent way to get my art noticed, but she told me she wasn't interested. She really was a terrible snob. She informed me her grandchildren had produced superior work when they were still toddlers. Can you imagine?"

"I most certainly can't," Mrs Davenport said, with what Lilly thought contained a hint of true indignation. "She obviously didn't know what she was talking about. I would happily see more of your work. You deserve a show all of your own, as far as I'm concerned."

"I was contemplating doing some portrait work. Would you be interested in posing for me?"

"Me? Oh, it would be like a dream come true, Travis. I would love to."

"Wonderful. Perhaps we should celebrate our new found collaboration with something a little stronger than tea? What do you say? I believe there is a small bar in the buffet room."

"You've twisted my arm, dear boy. Perhaps a small sherry?"

Mrs Davenport turned to Lilly with a wink unseen by Travis and handed her the key to the costume room.

"You better have the key, dear. You go home and rest. I'm not sure how long I'll be."

Lilly watched as Travis stood up and offered his arm to Mrs Davenport. She took it with a smile and they both wandered away, talking animatedly.

* * *

LILLY MADE HER WAY back down to the wardrobe room with Travis's comments on her mind. She was still in awe of Mrs Davenport's acting skills. She'd really taken on a completely different persona once she'd changed into her disguise and never once had she faltered. Lilly had really underestimated her.

All the other judges had seen Travis's work for what it was and Lilly couldn't fault Annabelle for rejecting his request to display it in her shop. If his competition entry had been his best effort, then she didn't want to see his worst. Had he been holding a grudge toward Annabelle ever since he'd been rejected? She couldn't be sure. He'd appeared to be genuinely upset at her death. But perhaps he'd been waiting for an opportune moment to take his revenge?

And what about Annabelle's grandson? He'd swiftly turned from being a nice young man to rude and obnoxious. His sister had been in tears, but were they real tears of grief or were they faked? They both certainly had a motive if they'd been denied their inheritance. What had been the catalyst in their relationship with Annabelle that had resulted in such an act? Eddie had obviously inherited his artistic skill from his grandmother, and he had mentioned briefly that he'd left art school even though his Gran had wanted him to continue. Could that be the reason? But surely his decision to not continue his studies wasn't serious enough to warrant such a reaction? She needed to dig deeper and investigate what had really happened.

She could also be on the wrong track entirely. Perhaps

there was another disgruntled artist out there who Annabelle had insulted?

She unlocked the costume room and made quick work of removing her wig, glasses, and coat. She returned them all to their places, took off the earrings and wiped the lipstick from her mouth. Making a last-minute check in the mirror to ensure she was back to looking like herself, she relocked the room and decided to return to the Green Room. Surely the other judges would be back by now?

She was walking past the ladies when Susanna exited in a hurry, just narrowly avoiding crashing into her. It didn't take a detective to see the woman had been crying.

Chapter Ten

"SUSANNA, WHATEVER IS WRONG?"

"Oh, Lilly. I was hoping I wouldn't be seen in this state."

"Can I help? Do you want to talk about it?"

Lilly remembered Susanna had something about Annabelle earlier while they were in the Green Room, but they'd been interrupted and she hadn't had time to ask her about it. Perhaps she'd be more open now.

"I'm just upset about Annabelle and trying to keep my composure but failing miserably. I'm both a judge and the Mayor of this town and as such should really be seen in control, but I'm finding it difficult."

"I am as well."

"Of course you found her, didn't you? I'm sorry, I shouldn't be thinking of myself."

Lilly didn't know if Mable had also told everyone how jealous she thought Lilly had been of Annabelle and her new shop, so she wanted to steer clear of being the one who found her.

"Did you know her well?" she asked Susanna.

"Not really. I knew her through previous council events when my husband was mayor."

"Do you mind me asking, did something happen between the two of you? You mentioned something earlier."

Susanna paused. "Don't breathe a word of what I'm about to tell you, Lilly. Do you remember my nephew, Carl?"

Lilly did. Carl had been a prime suspect in a previous murder case, one which Lilly had subsequently helped solve. She nodded.

"How is he?"

Susanna sighed deeply, a severely etched frown marring her otherwise perfect features.

"He got himself into a bit of trouble several weeks ago. If I've told him once, I've told him a thousand times he cannot drink and drive. Even if he's only had a single pint or glass of wine. It reflects extremely badly on my office, not to mention endangers his own life as well as other road users and pedestrians. It's not as though he doesn't have other ways of getting from A to B. I've told him I'll pick him up if his mother isn't available, or he can get a taxi and I'll pay for it. He is extremely spoiled and squanders everything he earns, living far above his means. But what can I do? He's family. Anyway, he didn't listen, as per usual. Needless to say, he ended up crashing his car one night, and unfortunately it was into Annabelle's fence."

"Oh no," Lilly said. "What did you do?"

"I went to talk to her. Apologised profusely for what had

happened and offered to pay for a complete new fence, not just the small part Carl had smashed into. Do you know what she said?" Lilly shook her head. "She was canny and knew exactly what my position would be if word got out about what Carl had done. So she promised not to breathe a word on the proviso that I pushed through her planning permission for the shop and the relevant permits she would need. I knew what her intentions for the old building were and I welcomed them. Part of my campaign was built on upgrading that area, as you know. Her permissions would never have been denied, but thanks to what she now had on Carl and, by association, me, she got everything fast-tracked and would have been able to open much sooner. It was nothing less than blackmail."

"I'm really surprised to hear that," Lilly said. "From the way everyone talks about her, she was a selfless and well-loved member of the community. Obviously there's more to her character than people know."

"Oh, there is. She's not what people think, Lilly. Or rather, I should say, she wasn't."

Lilly wished Susanna hadn't given in to Annabelle's demands, but like she said, the permissions would have been granted in the relatively near future, anyway. She was more disturbed that Annabelle had been perfectly willing to use blackmail to get what she wanted. "Is Carl still working for you, Susanna?"

"Yes, but not in the same capacity. I've found him a position that keeps him both busy and out of trouble. I hit the roof after the debacle with Annabelle and made him pay for it himself. I think he learned his lesson. Fortunately, he missed the statues that were in her garden. She sculpted them herself, so I can only imagine how much she would have demanded if those had been damaged."

"A fortune I expect," Lilly said. "Her work is exquisite."

"I agree. I recognised her work as soon as I saw it here. Did you?"

"Yes, I did. It was a stunning piece. It will be difficult to be impartial when choosing the winners, but I intend to do my best."

"I wonder if her grandson has entered? I know Lady Gresham mentioned she'd seen him earlier, and of course he used to be in art school, but not anymore."

"Yes, I heard something about that. Do you know what happened?"

"Oh yes. He dropped out. That's why Annabelle wrote him out of her will. She was furious with him. I've no idea why he left, but apparently his sister sided with him, so she wrote her out as well."

"Good grief, Susanna. How do you know all this? From Meredith? She mentioned the same thing when we were all in the green room. I saw you nodding when she was telling us."

Now it had been confirmed, Lilly was back to thinking both grandchildren had a perfect motive for murder. And being at the event also gave them the opportunity.

"No, I didn't hear it from Meredith. I don't know who told her. I overheard Annabelle and her solicitor talking over lunch one day. They had no idea I was there. Her solicitor's advice was to sleep on it, think it over, and make sure it was what she really wanted. He thought she was making a foolhardy decision in anger. I've no idea if he's even got around to doing as she asked. These things take time and it wasn't long ago that I was privy to their conversation. The will might not have been changed and of course now she's dead. If it hasn't, then it never will be."

"So her grandchildren might not know of her intentions?"

"They might not, but I doubt she'd be able to stop herself from telling them. Especially since she was so angry. It's the sort of thing I'd have expected her to throw in their face during an argument. Whether or not they believed she'd do it is another matter."

So, Lilly thought, Eddie and Elisa could have killed their grandmother before the will was changed in order to guarantee they'd inherit. Or, knowing they'd actually been written out, could have done it as vengeance. She was still thinking about the siblings when Susanna tapped her shoulder.

"Lilly?"

"Sorry, I was miles away."

"I need to call the office. I promised to check in. Thank you for listening. I'll see you back in the Green Room shortly. Oh, and please keep all this between us."

"You know I will, Susanna."

* * *

LILLY DECIDED TO GO to the kitchen for a cup of tea and to see Abigail and Stacey before she ventured back to the rest of the judges. She was sorely in need of friendly faces.

"Lilly!" Exclaimed Stacey when she arrived. "What was that getup?" she burst out laughing. "I hardly recognised you. Cool wig and glasses."

"Yes, but you did realise it was me. How did you know?"

"It was difficult, but I know you really well. It was your ring actually. You always wear that gold band with the leaf motif."

Lilly glanced at her right hand. The ring had belonged to her mother, and she never took it off.

"That was very observant, Stacey. And then you went and told Abigail."

"Of course she did," Abigail replied, grinning. "I had to see it for myself. But your costume, although good, was nothing compared to what Mrs Davenport was wearing. Now that was masterful. She looked nothing like herself. It was only her shape and the fact she was with you that we even realised it was her."

"I know. She played her part to perfection as well."

"So you were obviously sleuthing," Stacey said. "What did you find out? Anything that will help?"

"You haven't told anyone you saw us, have you?" Lilly asked, looking at both women. They shook their heads.

"Of course we haven't, Lilly," Abigail said. "We know better than to give the game away. So, was it a productive ruse?"

"I did get some useful information, but I'm not much further forward in terms of finding out who killed Annabelle. I can't really say much more at the moment. Bonnie has sworn me to secrecy. She doesn't want anyone knowing I'm working with her or I could find myself in really serious trouble. I promise, when I can tell you, I will."

"But let us know if we can help, okay?" Stacey said, her pretty features marred with genuine concern for her boss and friend.

"I will. Thank you both. How are things going here? Do you have everything you need?"

Abigail waved her concerns away.

"We have everything in hand, Lilly. You just concentrate on finding out who was responsible for this appalling crime and clear your name."

* * *

LILLY HAD ALMOST REACHED the Green Room when Susanna approached from the opposite direction. She looked harried, but was more composed than she had been earlier.

"Is everything all right?" Lilly asked her.

Susanna sighed.

"I've just had a rather difficult conversation with the Police Chief."

Lilly's heart sank. This was the boss of Bonnie's boss. The big man himself. If he was calling the mayor, then the news couldn't be good.

"What did he say?"

"He wants answers. And he wants them now. In a nutshell, he thinks Bonnie is taking too long."

"What? But that's nonsense. It's only been a matter of hours. Does he have any idea how long it takes to investigate this kind of crime? Interviewing all the people present at this event and working out who was where at the time and proving alibis doesn't happen quickly."

Susanna raised her hands. "You're preaching to the converted, Lilly. You and I both know Bonnie will be meticulous in her investigation, but Annabelle Haines was a prominent member of Plumpton Mallet and, as is often the case in these small communities, the families are connected. I have fully explained the situation to him and done the best I can to persuade him to give Bonnie more time, but there's only so much I can do. Let us hope she finds the culprit quickly or she could be taken off the case completely."

Lilly felt sick at hearing this news. If Bonnie was replaced, then Lilly would have no one to work with who believed in her innocence. Not to mention her best friend's reputation would suffer greatly.

"Come on. We still have a job to do here. There's a hungry crowd of artists waiting to hear who has won the competition."

It was the last thing on her mind, but Susanna was right. They needed to get it over with, then she could concentrate on her investigation.

Chapter Eleven

APART FROM MABLE, all the other judges were back in
the room when Susanna and Lilly entered. Mrs Davenport gave her a wink and a small smile. She was back to
looking like herself again. They both wandered over to the
table pushed up against a far wall, away from the others, os-
tensibly to help themselves to a cup of tea.

"Mrs Davenport," Lilly whispered. "You were absolutely
marvellous! Thank you so much for your help."

"You're most welcome, Lilly. I admit to enjoying every
minute of it, the seriousness of the situation, not with-
standing, of course."

"You really should consider doing some acting, you know.
You'd be excellent on stage. I've never seen anyone take on and
become a character as well as you did today."

"Goodness, did you really think so? Thank you, Lilly.
Well, I shall certainly give it some serious thought. Was it of
any help?"

"It was. I couldn't have done it without you."

"Are you two ready?" Lady Gresham called out. "We're about to choose our favourites."

Lilly and Mrs Davenport returned to their seats, and the deliberations began. Lilly was relieved that no one had accused her of committing the crime. Perhaps Mable hadn't said anything after all?

"How does it work?" Lilly asked.

"In years past we have each written down our favourites. Mable has already given me hers as she is busy elsewhere at the moment, then we would discuss them. However, I think this year we might as well forget that part and just talk about the ones we like the best and discuss their merits and adherence to the theme. Is everyone in agreement?"

There were various murmurs and nods of assent, and the discussion began in earnest.

Once three winners in each age category were selected, along with the order in which they would be awarded the prizes, Lilly was voted as the one who would write down the names of the painting and the artists and seal them in the appropriate envelope.

They were just about to begin deliberating on the second group when Bonnie entered and asked to speak with Lilly.

Outside in the hall, Bonnie gave her an update.

"I've just come back from the morgue."

"You delivered the hairdryer?"

"I did. The official cause of death was a blow to the head, so it's definitely murder and it looks likely the hair dryer was the weapon of choice. It's been confirmed the red splatter was blood and not paint and the broken casing was a result of the impact with her skull. I'm waiting for additional information."

"What about fingerprints?"

"They're being lifted as we speak. What about you? Have you discovered anything while I've been out?"

Lilly explained how she'd bumped into Eddie and Elisa, Annabelle's grandchildren, and tried surreptitiously to discover if there had been an argument between them all.

"I was careful with what I said, but Eddie realised who I was and practically accused me of killing his Gran because I was jealous of her new shop."

"Oh, Lilly," Bonnie sighed. "Tell me you didn't mention Annabelle's will?"

"No, I didn't," she replied. But didn't add that if the siblings hadn't have walked away, she might very well have done so. "But I did find out that it was Annabelle's intention. Although it may not have been done yet. If that's the case, her old will, in which I assume the pair of them will get something, will still be the valid one."

"How do you know this?"

Lilly explained her conversation with Susanna.

"All right, thanks, Lilly. I'll get one of my team to delve further into what you've told me. If the kids did know about her intentions, then it's a motive. But I suggest you steer clear of them. I don't want you adding more fuel to the flames. Anything else?"

"Just one other thing."

It only took Lilly a few minutes to explain her and Mrs Davenport's subterfuge. She expected Bonnie to berate her, but to her surprise she laughed.

"I really wish I'd been here to see that. And no one else twigged who you were?"

"No. Well, Stacey and Abigail did eventually, but they'll keep quiet."

"Okay, well, no more. Keep your head down. I'll have a look into Travis Jones and the other artists. Jealousy is a dangerous emotion and can make people do irrational things. There's a reason envy is one of the deadly sins."

"I'm not entirely convinced it was Travis who killed her. He seemed genuinely upset when he spoke of her death. He might have been jealous of her work and her reputation as an artist, but I think he's too self centered to kill someone."

Bonnie nodded.

"Well, we'll see what the investigation produces. I'll let you know if anything turns up. How is the judging going?"

"We were just getting started when you arrived."

"You better get back to it, then. I'll see you later, Lilly."

* * *

LILLY REJOINED THE OTHERS somewhat reluctantly. She'd been thrilled when she'd first been asked to be a judge, but now she just wished for it to be over so she could get back to helping Bonnie unveil the killer among them. There was so much at stake, her freedom being the most important one, and she was finding it increasingly difficult to concentrate on such a mundane matter as winners of a local amateur art competition.

But the quicker she got on with it, the quicker she would be out of the room and back to investigating.

While she'd been talking to Bonnie, the others had, by a process of elimination, decided upon their choices for the next two groups. Lilly cast her eye over the lists and found she agreed with their assessment.

The next group was the sixty-year-olds and above. The final one and the batch with Annabelle's entry.

"I have to say, for me, Annabelle Haines's painting was the stand out winner," Lady Gresham said. "And not because of today's tragic circumstances."

Mrs Davenport and Susanna agreed with her. All eyes turned expectantly, and somewhat apprehensively if Lilly was reading their expressions correctly, to her.

"I agree. It was really well executed and spoke to the theme perfectly. I have no qualms at declaring it the category winner."

"Do you think we will be accused of letting it win because of what has happened?" Susanna asked.

Lady Gresham nodded.

"I'm quite certain there will be a small faction of both the artists and the audience who will think exactly that. However, taken on merit alone, I would have chosen it regardless, and anyone with an ounce of art knowledge will come to see it is the best in that category."

With the winner decided, they moved onto second and third place. It was one of the more difficult decisions of the day and resulted in much discussion. But in the end, they all agreed.

"Right, that's all of them," Susanna said, slipping the final category winners into the designated envelope before Lilly could do so. Obviously, she wanted the proceedings to be over as quickly as Lilly did. "If someone could call Mable and let her know."

"I'll send her a text," Lady Gresham said. "Well done, ladies, and thank you."

They all stood up and a moment later Mable entered, followed by Bonnie.

"I believe we have our winners?"

"We do," Lady Gresham said, handing the envelopes to a surprised Lilly.

She handed them over to Mable with a forced smile. There was no need to be rude to the woman, but she'd well and truly landed Lilly in it, and she was still annoyed. It would be better if she kept her mouth shut.

"Lilly," the woman said, taking her by the elbow and leading her away from the group. "I really am dreadfully sorry about what I told Detective Phillips. I realise I shouldn't have said what I did, but I was so shocked to see Annabelle lying there with you kneeling beside her, and when I was questioned, I just blurted it all out. It was nerves, I suppose. It's one thing to know our town's police force is protecting us, but quite another to be questioned by them in an official capacity due to a serious crime. I truly didn't think you'd be treated as a suspect."

So what on earth did you think would happen? Lilly thought. She nodded and told the woman she understood. Mable moved to the centre of the room.

"Thank you for taking the time to judge the competition entries today. Especially under such trying circumstances. I'm sure I speak for all of us when I say what a dreadful shock Annabelle's death has been. She was such a light in our community and an exceptional talent. She will be missed dreadfully. Now, I believe Detective Phillips would like a word."

Bonnie stepped forward.

"We've almost completed interviewing all the attendees and once the prize award ceremony is finished, people will be allowed to leave. However, I may need to talk to some of you again at a later date, so, as they say in the movies, don't leave town."

"Are you any closer to finding out who did it?" Lady Gresham asked.

"I'm afraid I can't discuss an ongoing investigation. Thank you."

She gave Lilly a purposeful look and left the room. Lilly followed.

"Bonnie, what's going on?"

"I'm sorry, Lilly, but as of this moment I still haven't found anyone else who could have killed Annabelle Haines."

"Which means I'm still the prime suspect?"

"As far as the scant evidence goes, then yes, I'm afraid you are. But not to me. I know you're innocent, my friend, but I need concrete evidence to prove you are. Right now I have nothing."

"And you're getting it in the neck from the powers above?"

Bonnie frowned.

"How did you know?"

"Susanna. She had a telephone call saying they were putting pressure on you to solve the case quickly and..." she trailed off. She didn't know if Bonnie was aware she'd be removed as lead detective if she didn't find the killer soon.

"They'd bring in someone else if I failed?"

Lilly nodded.

"I'm sorry, Bonnie."

"Don't worry about me, Lilly. I'm more concerned about you. If I'm removed, you won't have an ally."

"I'd already realised that. We need to find something that will exonerate me, Bonnie."

"I'm working on it. I just need time. The forensics may tell us something but it doesn't happen quickly. Look, go back in there and try to take your mind off it. You've done what you can to help. Let me do my job and I promise as soon as I know anything, I'll come and tell you."

She gave her friend a quick hug and walked away, leaving Lilly shell shocked. Bonnie wasn't one for shows of affection. That brief hug said more than words ever could. Lilly was in serious trouble.

Chapter Twelve

WHEN SHE REENTERED THE ROOM, Lilly found the judges discussing what was coming up during the event now the judging had been completed.

There was to be an auction with funds raised going to various local initiatives who were involved in Eco-friendly and green initiatives, and to provide the funds for an art scholarship for a promising young artist. Many local businesses had donated items, Lilly had donated one of her exclusive tea sets, along with some of her own tea blends. And some of the artists had donated paintings. Everything was currently being set up, although Lilly knew Mable would delay the start of the bidding until Bonnie gave her the go ahead.

She knew Bonnie was doing her best to try to find the real killer, but Lilly couldn't help feel unhappy and increasingly anxious at how things were going. She was still the number one suspect, hard as it was for her to believe. She just hoped some of the other members of Bonnie's team were working as hard as her friend to prove her innocence. If any of them thought for a moment she was guilty, then the real killer might very well get away with it.

"The most popular item in the auction is one of Annabelle's original works," Lady Gresham was saying as Lilly tuned back into her surroundings. "I'm just sorry she won't be here to see how much it raises."

"Perhaps we should name the scholarship after her?" Mrs Davenport said.

There were stunned gazes all round.

"What a brilliant idea," Lilly said.

"Indeed," Lady Gresham said. "Well done, Mrs Davenport. That's exactly what we will do."

A moment later there was a discreet knock at the door and Stacey entered, pushing a laden tea trolley. Lilly stood to give her a hand, but she'd hardly had a chance to move when two plain-clothes detectives entered. She recognised neither of them.

"Lillian Tweed?" the taller of the two asked.

"Yes, that's me," she said, thinking Bonnie wanted a word. She was shocked when he approached and took her by the arm.

"You're to come with us to the station."

"What? Why?"

"You're being brought in for questioning."

"You're arresting me?"

"Not yet, but you are to be questioned under caution. I advise you not to say anything more."

* * *

L ILLY WAS STUNNED. She couldn't take it in. As the officers guided her out of the room, she could almost feel
the shocked stares of the judges boring into her back. Stacey
followed them into the hall.

"Wait! You can't do this. Lilly is innocent. She hasn't done
anything wrong. You can't arrest her!" Stacey shouted, close
to tears.

"And who might you be?" the short, rotund officer
said.

"Stacey Pepper. I work for Lilly. She's my friend."

"Well, I suggest you go back to work unless you want to
join her at the station?"

Lilly was escorted out of the building, flanked by the two
officers, with Stacey bringing up the rear, still asking questions. She wondered where her mild-mannered American
manager had disappeared to, because she was currently being
followed by a tiger bearing teeth and claws.

"Where are you taking her?" Stacey demanded as Lilly got
in the rear of a police car. "Does Bonnie know what you're
doing? You can't do this. She has rights."

"Stacey, please," begged Lilly, before the door was shut.
"Go back and help Abigail. I don't want you to get into
trouble as well. It's a misunderstanding, that's all. I'll come
back as soon as I can."

"Lilly, will you be all right? Are you sure?"

"I'm sure, Stacey. Try not to worry. And tell Bonnie what's
happened if you see her. And Archie. Please find Archie."

That was all she had time to say before the car door was
slammed and they moved off en route to the police station.
Lilly turned to look out of the vehicle's rear window and

found Stacey standing on the pavement, staring after them, a mix of fear and anger on her face.

* * *

LILLY WAS ABSOLUTELY MORTIFIED at being stuck in the back of the police car like a common criminal. The crowd of people outside the venue had stared in astonishment as she was taken away and she could imagine the whispered conversations that were currently going on. '*No smoke without fire,*' they would be saying.

She considered for an instant bowing her head so she didn't have to look into the faces of the people she'd known all her life, many of whom were customers. Goodness knows what this would do to her business. But she was innocent. She wouldn't let them see her cowed and defenceless. She lifted her head and resolutely stuck out her chin. Trying to stop it from wobbling.

The journey to the police station was a short one but due to the influx of traffic because of the Art competition, she could have got there quicker if she'd walked.

Eventually, they turned into the car park at the back and entered the rear door. After relinquishing her handbag to a duty officer, she was escorted through another door and straight into a stark holding cell.

"Someone will come and get you shortly," the tall officer said and disappeared to the resounding clang of metal.

Lilly stared in dismay at the small concrete box she'd been placed in. There was a small window up high in the wall opposite the door and a concrete shelf which acted as a seat and probably a bed should an overnight stay be needed. No doubt that was a thin, damp and heavily worn mattress stored in a cupboard somewhere. Lilly shook at the thought of having to spend the night here.

She sat down and put her head in her hands, willing herself not to cry. This was not the time for tears. She took a deep breath, letting it out slowly. Then another, willing her pulse to slow. Eventually, her hammering heart found a gentler rhythm and the cold tingles of anxiety dissipated. Feeling more in control, her thoughts turned to Bonnie. Where was she? Why had she let it come to this? Where Lilly was now in a cell all but accused of murder when she was innocent? Bonnie had said she believed her. Had she changed her mind? No, surely not. Bonnie was her best friend, and they'd known one another for years. She couldn't possibly believe Lilly was guilty. There must be another reason why she wasn't here.

Suddenly she had a frightening thought, which took her breath away. What if Bonnie had been removed from the investigation because she was close to Lilly? If they believed her guilty, then they'd stopped looking for the real killer and were now concentrating on trying to find evidence that would convict her. No matter how tenuous. Everything could now be out of Bonnie's hands completely.

She got up and began to pace. One, two, three steps, and turn. One, two, three steps and turn. If she had been brought in for questioning officially, then they must not have anyone else under suspicion. She mentally kicked herself for not being in the company of someone else all the time. She wouldn't be in this predicament if she had. But then again, she had no idea she'd be needing an alibi.

She stopped in the middle of the cell and massaged her neck. She felt the beginning of a tension headache starting. Sometimes it was indicative of a full-blown migraine on the way and she couldn't afford to be paralysed with pain. She needed to think her way out of this nightmare.

She moved on to massaging her temples and eventually began to feel the tight vice around her head lift a fraction. After ten minutes, the worst was over and she sat down, closing her eyes. She needed to start at the beginning. From the moment she arrived at the art competition venue to see if she could pinpoint anything that may help her.

Chapter Thirteen

S HE WRACKED HER BRAINS. Was there something she'd seen or heard that seemed innocuous at the time, but with the power of hindsight, was suspicious? Apart from the run in with Annabelle's grandchildren and the conversation Mrs Davenport had overheard, both of which made her a little uneasy, there was nothing she could grasp in the way of concrete evidence.

Then again, here she was in a cell with nothing more than a bout of envy and the fact she'd discovered the body as evidence against her. It was circumstantial and they could hardly prove her guilt with only those bits of information to go on, especially as she was innocent. But then she remembered how many times she'd heard of miscarriages of justice. Where innocent people had been found guilty and thrown in prison only to be exonerated years later.

She got up and started pacing again. This was doing her no good at all. She was going round and round and getting nowhere. All she was doing was worrying herself sick. Where was her positivity? She needed to speak to Bonnie urgently. The worst thing was being stuck in a solitary environment with absolutely no clue as to what was happening outside.

She'd just about reached the limit of her endurance, emotionally exhausted, when there was the sound of a key in the lock. She turned to the door just as it swung open to reveal the rotund officer who had originally brought her in.

He looked her with such a stern countenance Lilly's heart contracted and cold fear pooled in the pit of her stomach.

"You're free to go," he said.

Lilly stared at him for a moment, hardly understanding what he was telling her. She'd been expecting to be questioned. Was it some sort of cruel joke to put her on the back foot? Or had Bonnie finally found the real culprit?

"What?" she asked lamely.

"You can go. Unless you want to stay?"

"No, of course not."

She followed him out into the hallway where he led her through the offices and working part of the building, to the front where an officer returned her handbag before opening the door to reception. There she found Archie. He took two strides and enveloped her in a bone-crushing hug. She clung to him, willing herself not to cry, but she couldn't stop the shaking.

"Are you all right, Lilly?"

"I am now. How did you get me released?" she whispered.

"Let's go outside, love, and I'll explain."

* * *

"**D**ID I THANK YOU for getting me out?" Lilly asked Archie.

They had walked the five minutes from the police station to the memorial garden at the end of the market square and were now sitting together on a secluded bench under the shade of the oak and pine trees.

"You did. Several times. But there's no need. I could hardly leave you languishing in jail, could I? I mean, what would that do to my reputation? I'm a senior crime reporter remember, having my significant other arrested and rotting in a prison cell would make me the butt of all jokes."

He gave her a look, eyes twinkling and mouth twitching. Lilly laughed.

"I'd hate to be the cause of your ruined reputation, Mr Brown. I can't believe Bonnie let this happen."

"She didn't know, Lilly. Stacey called me and told me what had happened. I was out of town on the trail of a fraudster, otherwise, I'd have been with you sooner. But I made sure to call Bonnie on my way back and give her a mouthful. I was short with her, which wasn't fair in hindsight. But I was worried about you. Anyway, she's been taken off the case as the senior investigating officer, although she's still involved on the sidelines, and a detective from a city station has been put in her place. It was him who demanded you be taken in for questioning. When I told Bonnie, she was absolutely livid on your behalf. Obviously, someone higher up the food chain had become impatient with Bonnie not getting immediate results and had taken action. There was nothing she could do. But she was prepared to go as high as she could and fight on your behalf, even at the risk of her job. I talked her down. I assumed that's what you'd have wanted me to do?"

"Of course it is. Thank you, Archie. I'm relieved. I would have hated the thought of my best friend being responsible for throwing me in a jail cell. So how did you get me released?"

"I went to the chief."

"The boss of Bonnie's boss?" Lilly said, eyes wide in surprise. "I didn't realise you moved in such exalted circles, Mr Brown."

Archie nodded.

"Oh, I hobnob with all the important people, don't you know," he replied in his best plummy accent. "Anyway, yes, that's the chap. We've known one another for years. Long before he was promoted to the top job."

"What did you say to him?"

"Quite a lot I won't repeat, but ultimately I threatened to write a no holds barred exposé of the wrongful arrest of a much-loved and important member of Plumpton Mallet's community. The short sightedness of the senior officers and the guarantee of suing the department. Basically, I was prepared to cause such a stink he had no choice but to back down. At the end of my tirade, I believe he did realise just how short they were of real evidence against you. However, I think I've probably burned that particular bridge. I asked him to reinstate Bonnie, but he flat out refused. Once this investigation is over, then she'll get her old job back. But until then, she's on the periphery."

"Then it's up to me to find out who did, Archie. I don't trust the idiot who replaced her, considering he thought I'd done it."

"It's not up to you, Lilly. It's up to *us*."

"You'll help me?"

"Of course I will. I want your name cleared and Bonnie back in her job as much as you do. Besides, this is what couples do. Now, tell me what you and Bonnie have learned so far."

* * *

"I'M NOT SUPPOSED to be working with Bonnie. How did you know I was?" Lilly asked.

"Telepathy."

"Ha ha. Let me guess, Stacey?"

Archie nodded.

"I just wished I'd been there when you and Mrs Davenport donned your disguises. I would have paid good money to see you as a red head and Mrs D as a femme fatale."

Lilly laughed.

"Believe me, Archie, wig, glasses and trench-coat notwithstanding, I did nothing. It was Mrs Davenport, who was the star. Goodness knows who she was channeling, but it worked. She had Travis Jones eating out of her hand. At one point, I thought he was going to invite her home to see his etchings!"

Now it was Archie's turn to laugh.

"He'd have got a shock when the wig came off!"

"She was brilliant, honestly. I've underestimated her, that's for sure. If she'd stop being such a gossip in order to appear important, she'd actually be good fun. I think there's a really nice woman beneath that desperate desire to fit in at all costs. It's mainly lack of confidence I think. But I'm going to see if I can help when all this is over. Assuming I'm not in prison, of course."

"That's my girl," Archie said. "Always thinking of others, no matter what mess you find yourself in. And don't worry about prison, it won't come to that. And if it did, I'll bring a cake with a file in it. I'll have to get Abigail to bake it though, as I'm pretty useless in the kitchen. So, did you find out anything useful?"

Lilly grinned, so thankful Archie was there to lighten the seriousness with his humor.

"Not really. Mrs Davenport overheard a conversation between some of the artists maligning Annabelle and her work, but didn't see who they were. The only thing she very briefly noticed was a yellow cravat being removed from the pocket of someone who was leaving. It was only a brief glimpse, and it turned out to be Travis. Hence the disguises. However, when her name was brought up in conversation later, he seemed genuinely distraught at her passing. Bonnie obviously questioned him and some of the other artists, but can't pin anything on any of them."

"And what are your thoughts about Travis?"

"Mixed. I don't think he can be ruled out yet. He was jealous of both Annabelle's glowing reputation in the art world, and of her work. I understand how envy and jealousy can get you into trouble. Look what just happened to me."

"Yes, but you're innocent," Archie said. "Perhaps Travis is too?"

"Yes, he might well be. There are others to consider."

"Tell me about them."

Lilly smiled. She was so grateful to have Archie to brainstorm with. They'd done it numerous times now, and she valued his insight. They worked well together.

"I hate to say it, but Susanna also had a motive."

"You mean Susanna, the mayor?" Lilly nodded. "That's a surprise, considering her recent history. Go on, tell me the rest."

"It has to be completely off the record, Archie. She swore me to secrecy. Asked me not to breathe a word of what she told me."

"All right. Pulitzer be damned. I shan't say a word."

Lilly laughed, then explained what Susanna had told her about her nephew Carl and his drink driving. His accident with Annabelle's fence and the conversation which culminated in Susanna being blackmailed.

"Well, I can certainly understand Susanna wanting to keep that little incident quiet, but blackmail is a bit strong, isn't it?"

"What do you mean, Archie?"

"Neither of us were there, Lilly, so I can only guess at what was said, but I'm more inclined to think it was a case of 'you scratch my back and I'll scratch yours,' from Annabelle's point of view. She possibly never even conceived that her request would be viewed as blackmail. She never struck me as the sort of woman who would steep so low as to deliberately extort favours like that. We know the permissions and licenses would have been granted anyway, so what does obtaining them a few months early really mean? Nothing in the scheme of things."

"When you put it like that, I can see the logic. But as soon as she'd told Annabelle what Carl had done, Susanna couldn't take it back. I think from her point of view she'd put herself in an untenable position whereby anything that Annabelle needed she would ask Susanna for or she'd run the risk of Carl's secret getting out."

"That's a fair point, but honestly, I don't think Annabelle was capable of such deceit. She was as honest and trustworthy as they come, Lilly. Temper aside, which I suppose you could put down to that good old chestnut artist's temperament. I mean, we all get angry at some point, don't we?"

"Okay, but Susanna didn't know that, did she? She could quite easily have believed the bribery would go on for years. All the time she's in office. With Carl still working for her. Which means she still has to be treated as a suspect."

Archie nodded.

"Yes, she does. Although I'd be surprised if it was her. She's also doing a great job as mayor. I'd hate to see anything cut her tenure short. Unless she is guilty, of course."

"She was definitely distressed at Annabelle's death. Which is a point in her favour" "

"Well, taking the broader view, some people are exceptionally good actors," Archie said. "We only have to look at our previous cases to see that. And the amazing Mrs D, of course. So is that it with regard to suspects?"

Lilly shook her head.

"No. Actually, it was also Susanna who put me onto the next two."

"Two?"

"Yes. Annabelle's grandchildren, Eddie and Elisa."

* * *

"OH DEAR," ARCHIE SAID. "It begins to get very murky and sordid when family are involved, doesn't it? Then again, the police are taught to look at family members first when it comes to violence and murder. Except today when they took you in, of course. These out of towners are obviously idiots. I suppose there was a family argument of some sort? And they must have been in attendance at the event today?"

Lilly nodded.

"Yes, to both. Eddie is an exceptional artist like is Grandma and has one of his paintings in the competition today. Susanna apparently overheard Annabelle talking with her solicitor about writing both him and his sister out of her will. They'd had a huge row when Eddie informed her he was dropping out of art school to go his own way. His sister backed him up and Annabelle took umbrage. Whether she threatened them with losing their inheritance, I don't know. But it was obviously her intention. However, Susanna said as these things take time, and as the meeting she overheard wasn't that long ago, it might be that the will hadn't been changed in time before Annabelle died. Her solicitor tried to get her to think about it a bit more. Let the anger subside before making a rash decision, which she may have regretted later."

"It still puts the grandchildren squarely in the suspect frame either way," Archie said. "Do you know the cause of death yet?"

"According to Bonnie, it was a blow to the head. We found a very heavy, vintage hairdryer with the case cracked and possibly blood splatter in the artist's lounge. He's compared it to

Annabelle's head wound and said it could very well have been the murder weapon. However, he's not confirming or denying anything before the full lab analysis has been done."

"I didn't realise there was an artist's lounge."

"No, neither did I. Although the room has many uses depending on what the event is. When the Amateur Operatics are putting on a show, then they use it.

"So, we have at least four suspects, none of whom can be ruled out. But what about the rest of those attending? Could it have been someone other than those four?"

"It could have been anyone, Archie. The room was being used for any of the artists to touch up their work before they displayed it. We think the hairdryer was being used to quickly dry the paint, so it was probably within view of anyone who went in there. Not just the artists."

"And all those four have motive and opportunity. And as for method, it doesn't take much skill or strength to wield a hairdryer."

"So we're no further forward. We need something else, and quickly if I'm to clear my name."

"Come on, let's go back and see what we can find."

Lilly took a deep, slightly shaky breath and stood up. She wasn't looking forward to going back to the scene of the crime. Especially considering she'd been unceremoniously escorted out to a waiting police car in full view of everyone not long ago. There'd be many there who would think her guilty regardless of the fact she'd been released. Mud sticks. Thank goodness Archie would be with her.

Chapter Fourteen

WITH HER HEAD HELD HIGH and clutching Archie's hand, Lilly ascended the steps and entered the main hall. There were a few glances in her direction, but most of the crowd were intent on the auction, where the last lot was just coming under the hammer.

She saw Stacey at the same time as Stacey saw her. The girl's eyes widened, and she came rushing over, throwing her arms around Lilly in a fierce hug.

After a short while, Lilly whispered, "You're breaking my ribs, Stacey," and the girl let go.

"I'm sorry. I'm just so pleased to see you. Archie, thank you for springing her from chokey!"

Archie and Lilly burst out laughing.

"Where on earth did you hear that word, Stacey?" Archie asked. "It's positively archaic."

"I've been brushing up on my British slang. I don't know why it's not still used, it's such a cool word. So what happened?" she asked, turning back to Lilly. "Was it awful?"

Lilly nodded.

"Yes, it was pretty bad. I was just locked in a cell and left. The worst thing was not knowing what was going to happen to me, or what was going on outside. My mind was conjuring up all sorts of worst-case scenarios. Thank you for finding Archie for me, Stacey. And for going to bat for me."

"Anytime. So, are you two back on the case now? Bonnie's around here someplace, but she's not in charge anymore."

"I know, Archie told me. If you see her, tell her I'm back, would you? We're going to see if we can find out anything that will help."

"Sure thing," Stacey said. "I'll just go and tell Abigail you're free. She's been worried sick. See you later."

Lilly and Archie moved to an unobtrusive position on the back wall where they could view the crowd easily, but do so without drawing attention to themselves. Casting her eye around the room, Lilly spied Susanna talking to Lady Gresham. She was smiling and nodding at something the other woman had said. She looked far more relaxed than the last time Lilly had seen her. Was that because she thought Lilly was currently sitting in a cell accused of something Susanna was guilty of?

Archie nudged her.

"Are those two Annabelle's grandchildren?" he asked, indicating a pair of youngsters next to the fruit bowl painting.

"Yes. Eddie and Elisa. That's his painting."

"They're practically children, Lilly. Surely they can't be guilty?"

Lilly shrugged.

"We only have to look at similar cases in the past to know

age doesn't mean a thing. Besides, look at them. They're laughing and obviously sharing a few jokes. That doesn't seem like two people in mourning for a grandmother who was murdered only a few hours ago. I'm growing very suspicious of the pair of them."

"Horrible as it is, I'm with you there. So can you see this Travis Jones chap around anywhere?"

Lilly stood on tiptoe so she could see over the crowd of heads. Eventually, she found Travis. He was beside his own entry, arms waving expansively as he no doubt waxed lyrical about how crayon art was the future. She pointed him out to Archie, who couldn't help but grin.

"That's his art? What's the title, Toddlers and Tantrums?"

Lilly laughed.

"He's missed a trick if it isn't. But all joking aside, Mrs Davenport genuinely liked it and there are probably a few others it appeals to."

"Mmm," Archie said, unconvinced. "It takes all sorts to make the world go round, I suppose. We have a good vantage point here, with all the suspects in our sights. I suggest we stay here and see what transpires. What say you, Miss Tweed?"

"Here, here, Mr Brown. I do believe Mable is about to announce the winners."

"This should be interesting," Archie said, and Lilly silently agreed.

* * *

M ABLE ASCENDED THE STEPS to the stage where a microphone had already been positioned. She leaned forward and tapped it, causing a loud squeal of feedback that reverberated around the room.

"Goodness, I do apologise," she said to the audience, most of whom had their hands over their ears. She adjusted the microphone and stepped back slightly. "That's better, is it?" she asked the stage hand who gave her a thumbs up in response. She turned back to the crowd. "Well, now I have your attention it's time to announce the winners of this year's Amateur Artist competition. The entrants this year have been truly outstanding and as such, it has been an exceptionally difficult process to choose first, second and third places in each category. You really are all such talented artists and each of you are winners in my book. However, after much deliberation, the votes were cast and I have here in my hand the results." She shook the sheaf of envelopes she held and there was a smattering of applause. "Now, before I make the announcements, I would like to say a few words about the sudden and shocking loss of our dear friend Annabelle Haines."

As Mable continued, Lilly and Archie kept their eyes on the suspects. Eddie and Elisa were both wiping tears from their eyes. Lilly couldn't determine if they were crocodile or genuine and they were too far away for her to hear their conversation. Travis looked devastated and Susanna was valiantly trying to hold back the tears. She looked at Archie, who shrugged. None of their potential culprits were behaving abnormally. Lilly tuned back to Mable's speech. She was about to announce the winners.

"The first age group is the 16 to 24-year-olds." She tore

open the relevant envelope and announced the winners in reverse order. Serenity in third place, Abstract Eve in second. She paused for dramatic effect before announcing the victor. "The winner is 'Still Life in Wooden Bowl,' by Annabelle's grandson, Eddie."

There was a rapturous round of applause as Eddie pumped his fist in delight. He bounded up to the stage to receive his prize, a huge grin on his face. He approached the microphone.

"This is for my grandmother. Annabelle Haines."

The applause continued as Eddie left the stage and returned to his sister.

The announcements continued with the artists going up on stage to receive their prizes, and have their photographs taken for the PR that would follow. Then came the turn of the forty to sixty-year-olds.

"Is this the group Travis Jones is in?" Archie asked Lilly.

"Yes. You can see how excited he is. I'm sure he thinks he's going to win."

"And as a judge, you know otherwise?"

Lilly smiled.

"Nice try, Mr Brown, but I'm not allowed to give away that sort of information."

"Spoilsport," Archie replied with a grin.

Once again, the winners were announced in reverse order and Lilly and Archie, both watched Travis straighten his yellow cravat and brush the creases from his jacket in anticipation of going on stage. Mable cleared her throat.

"And the first prize goes to Angela Montgomery for her superb painting of otters underwater."

While Angela was accepting hearty congratulations, Lilly watched one of Travis's friends lay a sympathetic hand on his arm. He scowled and shrugged it off. Folding his arms.

"Oh dear," Archie said. "He's a bit of a sore loser. Mind you, I can't believe he truly thought melted wax crayon would win compared to the other entries."

Lilly frowned as something tickled the back of her mind, then disappeared as Mable began her final announcements.

The third place winner was one of Lilly's customers and she joined in the applause as she took the stage. Second place was awarded to one of Lilly's favourite pieces. That only left first place.

"And now the final award," Mable said, pausing for effect. The crowd grew quiet. "This means a great deal to me, as I'm sure it does to you all, too. Awarded posthumously, the first prize goes to Annabelle Haines."

The room erupted as the audience broke into cheers. Clapping loudly as the winning painting was set on a waiting easel placed centre stage. Eddie and Elisa were clapping along with the rest and wiping tears from their cheeks. They looked genuinely happy their grandmother had won.

Lilly turned just in time to see Travis storm from the room. Archie looked at her, eyebrows raised. He'd seen him too.

"Come on," he said, taking her arm. "Let's see where he's going."

Chapter Fifteen

I T WAS OBVIOUS that Travis had had enough of the art competition, but no one else had seen him leave except Lilly and Archie, intent as they were on the prize giving.

Lilly had expected Travis to leave the building, but as they followed, she saw him turn in the opposite direction down the long hallway. He was muttering to himself, although she couldn't hear the words.

They crept forward, trying not to give themselves away. At the end, they stopped and peered round a corner just in time to see him duck into an open doorway. Lilly grasped Archie's arm.

"I think I know where he's gone," she whispered. "I'm sure that's the artist's lounge. We need to be careful."

Lilly tiptoed forward, Archie right behind her. As they approached the open door, Lilly turned her head to Archie and put a finger to lips. He nodded in understanding. Lilly held her breath and peered around the door frame. The room was empty.

"That's strange," she said. "I was sure he came in here."

"You only saw him from the far end of the hall. He must have gone through another door. So this is where they touch up their work before displaying it?"

Lilly nodded. Everything looked the same as when she'd last seen it. Open jars and abandoned rags, with the scent of turpentine and linseed oil heavy in the air.

"What's this?" Archie asked, approaching a canvas with green smudges in one corner.

"Bonnie told me Annabelle had green paint on her hands. She thought she'd started something new just before she was killed."

Archie leaned in closer, tilting his head.

"Does that look like the start of a word to you?"

Lilly inspected what she'd assumed earlier was a cross. Then tilted her head as Archie had done. Suddenly it looked more like a letter T. The rest she couldn't make head nor tail of, but could the first part stand for Travis? If he was the murderer, then they'd need to prove he'd used the hairdryer. But did he grab it because it was the nearest thing to hand? Or had he been using it when Annabelle turned her back on him, giving him the opportunity?

"What would Travis be using a hairdryer for?" she mused out loud. Then she suddenly realised. "Of course! He didn't use paint so didn't need it for drying. He used crayon, which he melted using the heat from the hairdryer."

"Oh, Lilly, you know what this means, don't you?"

"Yes. Travis killed Annabelle."

Suddenly there was a noise and Lilly turned just in time to see Travis materialise from behind the open door where he'd been successfully hidden, give Archie a tremendous blow across the back of his head with a heavy frame and leg it out of the door.

Archie collapsed to the floor in an instant and Lilly screamed.

* * *

"ARCHIE," LILLY CRIED in floods of tears.

She was kneeling beside him, cupping his head in her hands. She felt the warm, sticky blood seeping through her fingers and grabbed a roll of kitchen paper from a nearby table. Wadding it up, she pressed it tightly to the wound to staunch the flow.

"Archie, can you hear me? Please wake up."

Suddenly, he groaned and opened his eyes.

"Hell's teeth. My head hurts. What happened?"

Lilly smiled through the tears.

"Travis was hiding behind the door and gave you a belt across the head. You're bleeding, Archie. You need to go to the hospital to get looked at and stitched up."

Archie sat up.

"Where's Travis now?"

"He ran out."

"Go after him, Lilly. Quickly. You can't let him get away and I'm fine, honestly. Head wounds bleed a lot. It looks worse than it is."

"Are you sure, Archie?"

"Of course. He killed Annabelle. He needs to be stopped before he escapes. Go on, I'll be right behind you."

"Keep pressure on that wound, Archie. You need to stop the bleeding."

Lilly grabbed his cheeks and gave him a quick but passionate kiss before running out of the door and down the hallway. Dashing tears from her cheeks and eyes as she pelted back to the main room.

She staggered through the door in time to see Mrs Davenport grab Travis's arm, preventing him from exiting.

"Stop him!" Lilly yelled. "He killed Annabelle. Travis Jones killed Annabelle Haines."

There was a split second silence from the gathering crowd. Then Eddie, realising what Lilly was saying, launched himself at Travis and rugby tackled him to the floor. There was a brief scuffle while Travis tried to get away, but he was no match for the younger, fitter man and eventually gave up.

"What's going on?" a voice said. Lilly turned. It was Bonnie.

"Bonnie! Thank goodness you're here. You need to arrest Travis Jones. He killed Annabelle. His finger prints will be on the hairdryer. We were just in the artist's lounge when Travis slugged Archie across the head and ran."

Bonnie nodded to one of her officers to deal with Travis, then turned to Lilly.

"Where is Archie now?"

"I'm here," a voice said behind them.

There were gasps from those closest who could see clearly the blood-soaked paper Archie clutched to his head. The blood had dripped down his neck and stained the collar, shoulder and half of the back of his shirt bright red.

Bonnie frowned and approached.

"Let me have a look." She gently lifted the paper away from the congealing blood. "It's almost stopped bleeding, and the laceration isn't too deep, but you're definitely going to need stitches, Archie, and you'll probably have a headache for a few days. The important thing is to keep an eye on you in case of a concussion. You need to get to the hospital."

Archie started to nod, then thought better of it as his eyes swam and the dizziness started.

"I'll take you, Archie," Lilly said.

"No, you need to stay with Bonnie and tell her what happened. I'll find another solution."

"One of my officers will take you," Bonnie said. "You can give him your statement at the same time. Off you go."

Lilly approached and gave him a hug.

"Don't play the hero, Archie. If the doctor insists on keeping you in overnight, then don't argue. Just text me and let me know one way or another, and I'll come over after I've finished here."

"Yes, you're probably right. I'll see you later, love. And if you get a chance, give Travis Jones a good old thump from me, will you?"

Lilly smiled.

"I'll see what I can do."

Lilly watched as Archie was gently led from the room by a uniformed officer, then turned back to Bonnie. She had an arrest to make and Lilly wanted to be there when it happened.

* * *

L ILLY FOLLOWED BONNIE to where Travis was now handcuffed and under the guard of a police officer. Eddie was standing to one side with his sister and another officer, who was ready to spring into action should the siblings decide to lunge at the man who had killed their grandmother.

"Why did you do it?" Lilly asked Travis. "What had Annabelle ever done to you? Was it her success as a such a fine artist that made you jealous enough to take her life?"

"Fine artist?" Travis scoffed. "Give me a break. She was so stuck in the past, churning out clichéd and derivative work, she wouldn't have known decent talent if she fell over it."

"That's not true!" Eddie shouted.

"What do you know?" Travis shot back. "You're still painting fruit in a bowl."

"Maybe, but I just won first prize in case you didn't notice."

"My work will live on, unlike yours. I didn't want my work displayed in her stupid shop, anyway."

"So that's why you killed her," Bonnie said. "She refused to put your work in her gallery."

"It was an accident."

Lilly shook her head, but kept her mouth shut. If it was an accident, then he'd have been more likely to come forward. But he hadn't. He'd deliberately hidden the murder weapon, then left the room and carried on as normal. Those were not the actions of a man fearful of having killed someone, but of one who had deliberately caused harm.

"Take him away," Bonnie said to her officer.

Suddenly, Mrs Davenport pushed through the crowd and marched up to Travis. She looked him straight in the eye, then slapped him hard across the cheek. "How could you?" she spat. "And to think I told you how much I admired your work."

Travis stood gaping, a red, hand-shaped welt rising on his cheek.

"I don't even know who you are, you stupid old hag."

Lilly smiled. The only time he'd seen Mrs Davenport was in her disguise. Silently, she cheered her action. Archie would be pleased someone had given Travis Jones a little of what he deserved.

While Travis was being escorted out of the building kicking and screaming, Bonnie approached Lilly.

"Well, it looks like I have my man. It's good to see you walking about again, Lilly. I'm so sorry it ended up like that. It was totally out of my hands. I had no idea what had happened and by the time I did, I was told in no uncertain terms to stay out of it. I couldn't even come to the station to see you or I'd have risked my job."

"It's all right, Bonnie, honestly. Archie explained what had happened. Are you back in charge now?"

"Sort of. Or I will be once the idiots upstairs realise we've made an arrest. The right person this time."

"Yes, that helps," Lilly said. "I don't ever want to have to go through that again, Bonnie. It was awful. The worst thing was being kept in the dark and not knowing what was happening."

"Miss Tweed?"

Lilly turned and came face-to-face with Eddie and Elisa.

"Yes?"

"I'd like to apologise," Eddie said and his sister nodded in agreement. "I shouldn't have been so rude to you. Or accusatory. I see now that you were just trying to get to the truth."

Lilly nodded. "Thank you. I know how difficult it must be for you. All our emotions were running high today. I'm just glad we found out who did it. I know it's not much consolation considering your dreadful loss. Will you both be all right?"

Eddie nodded. "We have our family. Thank you again."

Lilly turned to Bonnie.

"Do you need me here, Bonnie?"

Bonnie shook her head.

"No. You go to the hospital and check on Archie. I'll pop by and take your official statement when you're back home."

Lilly thanked her and dashed out to her car. The only place she wanted to be was by Archie's side.

Chapter Sixteen

I<small>T WAS SEVERAL DAYS LATER</small> and Lilly was currently viewing herself in the full-length mirror in her bedroom. She was wearing her one and only little black dress, but wondering if it was too austere for the occasion. Considering what had happened, she didn't want to look as though she were attending a funeral.

"No, it won't do, Earl," she told the cat who was eying her from the bed. "I need something colourful and joyful to celebrate a creative life."

She pulled the dress over her head and hung it back up. Sliding the hangers along the rail, she perused what she had.

"Ah ha! This will do perfectly."

It was a vintage designer dress she'd picked up in Covent Garden a few years ago. Mid sleeve, mid-length and in colours of cream, teal and dusky rose. She'd pair it with her long velvet coat, another vintage favourite.

She glanced at her watch. It was time to leave. She scratched Earl's head, eliciting loud purrs, and left him on the bed.

She'd just started her car when she received a text from Archie checking she was on her way. He was already at the venue with his reporter hat on. Literally as it happened, as he needed something to cover up the ugly stitches in his head wound. She replied in the affirmative and backed the car out of the drive. She was looking forward to this event. Not least because she was there as a guest, not as the caterer. She didn't get the chance often.

The sun was just setting as Lilly parked her car on the outskirts of town. The sky was a riot of purples, oranges, and violets. *It looks like a painting,* Lilly thought. Very apt considering where she was going. Annabelle's tea shop. Except it was no longer a tea shop. Tonight was the grand opening of Plumpton Mallet's newest art venue; The Haines Gallery and artist's studio.

* * *

S HE OPENED THE DOOR and walked in. She didn't have time to close it before Archie was by her side, two glasses of chilled wine in his hands.

"Good evening, Miss Tweed. I must say you're looking delectable. I don't think I've seen this particular outfit before."

"Hello, Archie," Lilly said, responding to the brief kiss before taking a glass. "You must recognise the coat. I wore it on our train trip."

"Oh, I do. I was talking about the frock. Is it new?"

Lilly smiled at Archie's old-fashioned word usage.

"No, not new. I've just not worn it for a long time. You're looking very dapper as usual, Archie."

He had on a linen suit in forest green, paired with a cream shirt and beige and white horizontal striped tie. His waistcoat was in a darker green, threaded with gold. His shoes were suede bucks in beige. And his head was covered in a beige panama with a deep green band.

"Oh, this old thing," he replied with a wave of his hand, followed by a wink.

Lilly laughed. No doubt he'd bought it just for the occasion. Archie Brown loved his clothes.

"Come on, we best mingle," Lilly said.

"Indeed. Although as I'm officially on duty, I'll have to leave you shortly."

Eddie and Elisa had been impressed with the article Archie had written about their grandmother's death. He'd included a beautiful tribute to Annabelle and when they'd announced their intention to do away with the tea shop and instead turn her vision into a dedicated art gallery showcasing local artist's work, and hiring out the rear spaces for studios and for teaching workshops, they'd specifically asked that he be the one to write about it. Archie was more than willing to oblige.

Ten minutes later, Lilly went to catch up with her colleagues and friends while Archie went into reporter mode. First, she went to congratulate Eddie and Elisa.

"I'm sure Annabelle would be very proud you're both taking over the gallery. You've already achieved so much since my last visit. It looks wonderful."

"Thank you. There were already a number of artists Gran was showcasing, but now we're not doing the tea side of things, it means we have more room. We had a difficult time winnowing down the list of people who wanted to display their work, actually. But we're doing it on a rotation basis initially, so everyone gets a fair shot."

"I'll be running it mostly myself," Elisa added. "Because Eddie has decided to go back to art school."

"That's great news," Lilly said.

Eddie nodded. "It's what Gran wanted. I'll be doing it in her memory. And in my spare time, I'll be helping here."

Lilly congratulated them again, then went in search of Stacey and Abigail. She found them sampling the buffet and comparing them with the Agony Aunt's cafe recipes.

"Who's winning?" Lilly asked, laughing.

"We are, of course," Abigail said. "But it's certainly given me a lot of ideas."

They chatted for a few minutes more, then Lilly spied Bonnie at the same time Bonnie noticed her. They moved to a relatively clear space where they wouldn't be overheard. This was the first time since Travis Jones had been arrested that they'd had a chance to speak.

"So, are you back in the driving seat again, Bonnie?"

"I am. And with an apology would you believe? Whatever Archie said did the trick with bells on."

"As far as I can gather, there were some veiled threats pertaining to not very favourable articles appearing in the paper, along with a possibility of legal proceedings."

"Good for him. They needed taking down a peg or two."

"He was furious for us both. I'm just glad he was on our side. So, what's happening with Travis Jones?"

"He confessed."

"So it wasn't an accident like he said?"

"Oh no, he meant her harm all right. Although whether his

intention was to kill her will be up to the jury. Apparently, he was in the artist's lounge alone when Annabelle came in. She'd had an idea which couldn't wait and she needed to get it on canvas. Travis was using the hairdryer to melt his crayons and mentioned he'd be willing to display his work in her new gallery, for a fee."

"He wanted her to pay him?" Lilly asked in amazement.

"He thought he was doing her a favour. Anyway, she turned him down flat. Said his work wasn't up to the standard she envisioned for the space. In his own words, he saw red and he used the nearest thing to hand to attack her."

"The hairdryer."

"Right. Which he then hid behind the desk where you found it and went about his business as though nothing had happened."

"So it wasn't premeditated."

"No. Spur of the moment through a fit of anger and jealousy. Namely, loss of control. Which means he's likely to get voluntary manslaughter."

"What does that mean in terms of his sentence?" Lilly asked.

"It will depend on the judge and whether Travis pleads guilty. Life is the maximum a judge can impose, but if he pleads guilty, that could be reduced by about a third. Either way, he's going to prison for a long time."

Lilly shuddered. She'd only been locked up in the local police station's cell for an hour or two and found it unbearable. She couldn't imagine what Travis Jones would feel like. But then again, he had taken someone's life.

"Lilly, I think you're wanted," Bonnie said, indicating behind her.

Lilly turned to find Abigail coming towards them with a large platter filled with various desserts.

"Lilly, look at these."

"They are beautiful, Abigail."

"What do you notice about them?"

"They are very flowery," Lilly replied. "Is that what you meant?"

"Almost. Yes, they are decorated with flowers, but they are real. Edible flowers, isn't that amazing?"

Lilly grinned. "You've had an idea, haven't you?"

"I have. Now, wait until you hear my plan."

Lilly smiled at Bonnie. It looked as though The Tea Emporium and The Agony Aunt's cafe had another special event to cater in the very near future.

Did you enjoy Green with Envy? It would be lovely if you could leave a brief review on the site where you bought it. It really helps other readers to find the books. Thank you.

*

FREE BOOK – The Yellow Cottage Mystery, the prequel short story to J. New's British historical mystery series, is yours as a thank you for joining her Reader's Group newsletter. You can find more information on the website: www.jnewwrites.com

*

Have you met Ella Bridges yet? England in the 1930s. **The Yellow Cottage Vintage Mysteries.** Immerse yourself in country house murders, dastardly deeds at English church fetes, daring escapades in the French Riviera and the secret tunnels under London, in the award-winning series readers call, 'Miss Marple' meets 'The Ghost Whisperer.'

THE BOOKS:
• An Accidental Murder
• The Curse of Arundel Hall
• A Clerical Error
• The Riviera Affair
• A Double Life

Available in book shops internationally in print, e-book and audio formats. Check the website for more information. www.jnewwrites.com

*

The Finch & Fischer Mysteries – this British contemporary cozy series features mobile librarian Penny Finch and her rescue dog Fischer as they sniff out red-herrings and dig up trouble in six local villages.

THE BOOKS:
- Decked in the Hall
- Death at the Duck Pond
- Battered to Death
- Fatality at the Fair

Available in book shops internationally in print and e-book formats. Check the website for more information. www.jnewwrites.com

About the Author

J. New is the author of **The Yellow Cottage Vintage Mysteries**, traditional English whodunits with a twist, set in the 1930s. Known for their clever humor as well as the interesting slant on the traditional whodunit.

She also writes the **Finch & Fischer** and the **Tea & Sympathy** mysteries, both contemporary cozy crime series.

Jacquie was born in West Yorkshire, England. She studied art and design and after qualifying began work as an interior designer, moving onto fine art restoration and animal portraiture before making the decision to pursue her lifelong ambition to write. She now writes full time and lives with her partner of twenty-four years, along with an assortment of stray cats and dogs they have rescued.

Printed by BoD™in Norderstedt, Germany

9 798223 352617